# THE DARKNESS OF WALLIS SIMPSON

# The Darkness of Wallis Simpson

## and other stories

Rose Tremain

Chatto & Windus
London

'How It Stacks Up' was first published as 'The Stack' in the *New Yorker* © Rose Tremain 1996. 'The Beauty of the Dawn Shift' was first published in *New Writing 5*, eds A. S. Byatt and Christopher Hope © Rose Tremain 1996. 'Death of an Advocate' was read on Radio 3's *The Verb* © Rose Tremain 2004. 'Nativity Story' was first published as 'One Night in Winter' in *Country Life* © Rose Tremain 1999. 'The Over-Ride' was first published in the *Sunday Express* © Rose Tremain 1999. 'Moth' was first published in *Good Housekeeping* © Rose Tremain 1998. 'The Cherry Orchard, with Rugs' was first published in *The Times* © Rose Tremain 2004. 'Peerless' was first published in *Prospect* © Rose Tremain 2005. 'The Dead Are Only Sleeping' was first published in the *Guardian* © Rose Tremain 2005

Lines from 'Singing the Blues', by Tommy Steele, © Sony/ATV Music Publishing

Line from 'Tonight I Can Write' from *Twenty Love Poems* by Pablo Neruda, published by Jonathan Cape. Reprinted by permission of the Random House Group Limited.

Published by Chatto & Windus 2005

2 4 6 8 10 9 7 5 3 1

First published in Great Britain in 2005 by
Chatto & Windus
Random House, 20 Vauxhall Bridge Road,
London SW1V 2SA

Random House Australia (Pty) Limited
20 Alfred Street, Milsons Point, Sydney,
New South Wales 2061, Australia

Random House New Zealand Limited
18 Poland Road, Glenfield,
Auckland 10, New Zealand

Random House (Pty) Limited
Endulini, 5A Jubilee Road, Parktown 2193, South Africa

The Random House Group Limited Reg. No. 954009
www.randomhouse.co.uk

A CIP catalogue record for this book is available from the British Library

ISBN 1 8605 6032 6

Papers used by The Random House Group Limited are natural, recyclable products made from wood grown in sustainable forests; the manufacturing processes conform to the environmental regulations of the country of origin

Typeset by SX Composing DTP, Rayleigh, Essex
Printed and bound in Great Britain by Clays Ltd, St. Ives Plc

# Contents

*For Vivien Green,*
*with love and gratitude*

The Darkness of Wallis Simpson

*Love is so short, forgetting is so long.*
                                    Pablo Neruda

They say she's gaga. That's the word she's heard them whispering. *Gaga*. It sounds like something a baby would say.

She knows she's in Paris, city of dreams. Her companion in the shadowy room, who kisses her forehead, who strokes her hands, keeps telling her that she has a duty not to die, not now, not *yet*. 'Wallisse . . .' murmurs this person, who smells like a woman with peppermint breath, but whose cheeks are hard as a man's. 'Wallisse . . . I shall not let you die until you remember.'

Remember what? There are plenty of questions Wallis would like to ask, but she can't get them out. What a bitch. Words compose themselves in her mind. They're in the proper order, usually. Except she can hardly ever say them. Her throat has a disease. What comes out of her mouth is dribble. Dribble and some droll, incomprehensible language. Afrikaans?

The woman-man companion lifts her up in the wide bed, cradles her against her anatomy, which is bulky-thick, like a bale of packed cotton, and begins brushing her hair. 'Beautiful . . .' whispers the bulk as she brushes. And

Wallis tries to say: 'Oh yes, it was always *very* becoming. In fact, it was my best feature, dark and sleek as a Shanghai girl's. It transfigured me. It sprang from blood. Not *my* blood. From the tumbler of raw-steak blood I was made to drink every day after school, to ward off TB, and my mother would say: "Drink it down, Bessiewallis. Make your tresses shine."'

But her sentences turn to goo. The stench of lilies is on the pillow. And the room is so damn dark – with just these thin movements in it, these shadows she can't make out – it's mortifying, like she's watching some old flickering TV picture, or even not watching, but trapped *inside* an old TV, a ghost made out of light, longing to join the world beyond the screen, the world of the TV watchers, pink as candy, warm and rounded, with their haunches nudging up close to each other on their chintzy divan. How comely these brightly coloured people seem! As if nothing cold would ever touch them. As if they would rise up in a line and dance a conga, hands-to-ass, hands-to-ass, swaying along, in and out of the furniture, singing sharp, singing flat, not caring a dime, untouched by tomorrow, heading pell-mell into the hall, waking the servants, opening the door and shimmying out under the summer moon.

Out where?

The companion has said in her strange, difficult-to-understand English: 'Wallisse, for you, this state of forgetting is a mortal sin. *A mortal sin!* Do you want to die with this stain of sin on your soul?'

'Stain of sin'. No, sure she doesn't want to die with this on her. It sounds revolting. But just what is it a girl's supposed to remember? She tries to say: 'I remember Baltimore in spring. Is that it?' But the companion never

4

answers. And now she's gone out the door, closing it, locking it, leaving Wallis alone, a prisoner. And the sound of that key turning, that's the lonesomest sound in the world, the one that can bring the Nightmare on . . .

Wallis clutches the bed sheet. Once, she hid her too-large hands in white gloves; now, her hands are small, like the claws of a marmoset – another mystery. She calls out: 'Don't leave me alone!' But she hears the sound she makes. Not proper words, just an oddball noise. Nobody's going to answer an animal noise. They'll assume wolves have come back to the Bois de Boulogne. The door remains tight shut.

And here comes the Nightmare. Always the same scene. Florida palms. A bright white glare on the edge of the veranda. And Wallis sits in a wickerwork chair, waiting. 6 Admiralty Row, Pensacola. Waiting for her husband to come home. 1916. Waiting with her arms folded, woollen dress neat, slip one inch and a half shorter than the dress, tortoiseshell barrette holding back the soft waves of her long lovely hair . . .

Waiting with such pride! Waiting to see his shadow moving ahead of him down Admiralty Row, moving towards her, she bandbox-smart as a US Navy wife should always be. When she met him, she cabled her mother in Baltimore: *Last night, I danced with the world's most fascinating aviator.* Poor schoolmates, poor debutantes of Baltimore, poor Mother, poor American girls everywhere, who'd never known the embrace of Earl Winfield Spencer Jr. And now he was hers, her husband, and any moment she would see him: gold stripes on his shoulder boards, dark moustache, sunburned skin. He would smile as he caught sight of her, his bride, his Wallis, who was teaching herself to cook from *Fannie Farmer's Boston Cooking School Cook Book*, who already knew how to season Campbell's soup and make a gravy without lumps, and who was progressing to omelettes and fruit pie.

But then. The bright glare of the sun on the veranda is gone. The sun's going down over the bay. The houses on the other side of Admiralty Row are already in deep shadow. The air is cooling. It's wintertime. And Fannie Farmer's perfect gravy can't be made yet because the fascinating aviator hasn't come home.

At Pensacola Naval Air Station there is a gong which sounds whenever a plane goes down. A gong. As though a motion picture were about to begin, except there were no motion pictures then. But the base goes silent, and the wives put their arms round each other and you can smell their fear even through talcum powder, and all you can do is hold on, all you young wives together, with your hearts beating. Hold on until you know. And the wind blows. It seems always to be blowing sand in your eyes and you can hear it in the high palms: death trying to flirt with the leaves.

But the gong doesn't sound that evening. It gets dark and Wallis goes inside and takes the joint of beef out of the oven and stares at it, the yellow fat turned brown, blood in the pan. She doesn't know what to do to prevent it from spoiling, so she places it on the draining board. And then she realises she is cold, the night is cold, and she goes towards the bedroom to find a shawl, a white one, which will complement her beige-and-brown dress.

She never reaches the bedroom because Win is at the front door. She can hear him jabbing at the lock with his key and she knows what this means.

6

When they checked in at the Greenbrier Hotel, White Sulphur Springs, on the first night of their marriage, Win ordered whiskey to be sent to the room, but the desk clerk said: 'I'm sorry, sir, but West Virginia is a dry county.' And Win cursed, he cursed like the devil. He said: 'Imagine this happening to a man on his honeymoon!' and took out of his suitcase a silver flask and sank into an armchair and drank, drank every drop in the flask, and Wallis tried to protest: 'Win, you're hurting a girl's feelings kissin' that ole flask when you could be kissin' your bride . . .' And he told her: 'Don't you dare. Don't you *ever* tell a man what he should or should not be doing.'

Win's breath is fiery and scorches her face, but the rest of her is shivering.

Why didn't she get the shawl from the closet? Because she ran to the door, to open it for Win, to say: 'Oh, Win, I pictured you dead! I was listening out for the gong.'

His white uniform is stained yellow down the front. His eyes are huge and wild. 'Listening out for the gong? Guess you want me dead then? Bet you darn well do.'

'Oh, don't say that . . .'

'Might as well be dead as live with you. Frigid bitch.'

He shoulders her aside and goes to the kitchen and she follows and he opens the refrigerator and takes out a jug of milk and begins drinking from the jug. Then he sees the meat on the draining board and says: 'What's that hunk of excrement?'

'Win,' she says, 'that's our dinner. I'm going to make a gravy . . .'

'Past tense,' he says. 'I'm not eating that.' And he takes up the joint, dripping with its half-cold fat, and hurls it at her. She ducks, but it slams into her head, bruising her ear, spoiling her carefully arranged hair. And this makes her mad. Mad at him for not seeing what a good wife she's trying to be – with her cooking, with her neat appearance, not to mention doing *that* for him when all it does is burn her, burn her inside – and so she flies at him and beats on his chest with her fists. He's her husband and he never treats her like a wife and this makes her so mad, so mad and sad. But he's a strong man. He grabs her arms. He twists them round, like he's trying to snap them, her thin arms in the wool dress. She begins screaming, but it doesn't move him. He pushes her forward, kicking her legs, making her walk.

His hand, which stinks of something bitter, is now over her mouth. Within the cage of his reeking hand, her screams die. How could marriage be *this*? She'd worn a gown of white panne velvet with a bodice embroidered with pearls and a petticoat of heirloom lace. A long court train had fallen from her shoulders. A coronet of orange blossoms had circled her lovely hair . . .

Win picks her up now, as they go into the bathroom. He dumps her in the cold white tub. There's pain in her spine. She's crying and pleading: 'I'm your wife . . . I'm your wife . . .' He holds her body down in the tub with one foot, his shoe heavy on her stomach. He unbuttons his fly. She screams louder, covers her face. His burning urine drenches her. She gags. She's the wife of an animal. But how can this be, when, at the altar, he'd looked so much like a handsome man, when, as she moved down the aisle towards this smart and upright groom, she'd carried a bouquet of white orchids and lily of the valley, tied with white silk ribbons . . .? She cries without ceasing. She thinks she'll never stop crying as long as she lives . . .

*

Then comes the night. Lying in the bathroom in her soaking dress. Sick and shivering. Alone. Alone as she has never been. Alone in the dark, because Win tore out the bulb from the light, grabbed the key, turned it in the lock. Alone for ever? For why should a man who could do this to her ever come back to rescue her?

He took away the towels. She can't dry herself, can't wrap her body in anything. She removes her dress and her underwear (which she washes every day in soap flakes, to make sure that a young bride is always clean and fragrant), runs hot water and climbs back into the tub and lies without moving, feeling warmth returning. But the water cools. She runs more. This cools in its turn. Wallis gets out and lies down on the bath mat, tries to wrap herself in the mat, which is worn and grey. She's twenty-one years old. Far away in Europe, men are dying in a war that seems to have no end. She wishes that Winfield Spencer would fly there and crash his plane into the snow and that bits of his body would be scattered in pools of blood over the hard crust of northern France.

Her Nightmare's like a war. It has no end. It's followed her through all her years since 1916. As though this was what she *deserved*, as though society had decreed: Bessiewallis, née Warfield, daughter of lovely Alice Montague and poor sickly Teackle Warfield who died of a consumption before his daughter could say his peculiar name, this pretty Bessie with her violet eyes, this girl with a cow's name is going to be cowed with shame. Men will spit on her. And worse. And at the end of it all, she'll be quite alone.

Wallis longs to sleep. Though the bedclothes weigh her down, because she's barely made of soft flesh any more, just sinew and bone, Wallis can sometimes drift off to sleep on some comforting tide of thought. And here comes one: she's in Baltimore, in the yard of her grandmother's house, 34 East Preston Street. She's fourteen or fifteen. She wears a bright ribbon in her dark hair. (Her Uncle Sol calls her 'Minnehaha'.) She's helping Ruby, the coloured maid, to hang up sheets in a salt wind, in that wind from the sea which is so beneficial to the lungs, which should be breathed ninety-nine times a day to keep away the Disease that must not be named any more.

Obediently, she's breathing. The wind moves in the big linden tree, with its dear little buds of leaves not open yet. Gulls swoop round, up there in the blue Baltimore sky. The linen sheets on the line keep blowing against Wallis's body, like a touch from someone else, and this is so nice, it's almost wonderful. You could write a poem about this feeling, if you could make the words say what you felt.

At lunch, she asks her grandmother: 'Could I write a poem, Grandma?'

'Sit up, Bessiewallis,' her grandmother replies. Then, after some time and with a sniff, she declares: 'Writing is very bad for the deportment. Luckily, not many women do it. In America, we leave poetry to the men.'

Grandmother Anna Emory Warfield holds herself so ramrod straight in her chair that not one inch of her spine touches the chair back. And she wants Bessiewallis to follow her example, to respect her Southern heritage, to remember she's a lady, to try never to be dull, to strive to be witty, yet to watch others, learn from them, listen to them, draw them into conversation: 'That way, you will be a good hostess one day, dear, and preside over a dazzling table.'

A dazzling table? Bessiewallis imagines a million twinkling and flickering candles; yellow flames licking the glassware, wax pooling and dripping and falling into the soup, the tablecloth catching fire . . .

'Where will this dazzling table be?' she enquires. And sees a rare smile cross the face of Anna Emory Warfield.

'Where will it be? Why, I couldn't tell, dear. Except it will surely be in the South. It would never do to marry a Yankee.'

Marriage. It's the word on everybody's mind. And time is flying, swooping like the gulls. That's what the grown-ups keep implying. Not a moment to spare for poetry. No time for playing 'catch' with Ruby, in and out of the sheets on the drying line. No time for play of any kind. Her paper dolls, 'Mrs Astor' and 'Mrs Vanderbilt', with their paper wardrobe of cocktail gowns, are back in the dark and dust of her closet, together with all the other bits and pieces of her childhood. She thinks sadly of them sometimes, Mrs A and Mrs V, so lonely, without any soirées to attend. But still time keeps accelerating along, like the new motor cars on Preston Street. In three years, Wallis is going to be a debutante. She is going to wear a lace gown and dance at the Bachelors' Cotillion. And out of the crowd of tail-coated young bachelors, with their white ties and their nervous smiles and their hair sleek with pomade, there she will find him, the One and Only.

Lunch is over and now, as Bessiewallis steps out into the Baltimore sun, going to Richmond Market with her grandmother, morning arrives in Paris, first as a grey presence in the room, a thing which has barely decided to stay, and then as a shaft of light, gold and soft at the window, where the heavy drapes are drawn back an inch or two. Wallis looks at this shaft. She's slept and not dreamed. She feels a bit better. She can see the damned window perfectly clearly. She thinks she may be able to say a few words today, in sensible American.

The companion is there. Her skin's pale brown, freckled in places, and stretched taut and hard over her skull. She lifts Wallis up in the bed. Pulls up her nightdress. Some aproned and uniformed girl Wallis can't remember seeing before shoves a pan under her. '*Fais pipi, ma Duchesse,*' says the companion. '*Fais un petit pipi pour moi.*'

Oh, Gawd. French.

As though speaking weren't hard enough. Speaking American. As though this weren't taxing already.

'Speak English,' commands Wallis. And yeah, her voice is OK today. The woman-man smiles in surprise.

'Good,' she says. (She is a 'she', is she? Or a man in a costume? A man with a big chest?) 'I see my *Duchesse* is feeling herself again. Bravo. Very good. So now do your little tinkle, my dear, and then I 'ave some things to show you. Things to help you remember. Today, I think, is going to be the day when you understand again.'

Wallis stares at the companion. ('Never stare, Bessiewallis,' advises Grandma Anna. 'Because it's a low-down thing to do. If you wish to make some internal interrogation, just hold a face fleetingly with your eyes.' But what the hell. She's long dead, Anna Emory Warfield. Baltimore changed. From brown to grey. The linden tree was felled. Why not stare at everything that remains?) The companion's hair is short and thick and grey. Her hands look tough.

The aproned girl is going round the room, tidying what already looks tidy enough. She, at least, thinks Wallis, has the decency not to stare at me while I'm trying to piss. The companion is shameless, though. She's stroking my hand, kissing my hair, and all while I'm sitting on the fucking pan.

'Go away,' she says.

The woman-man looks so hurt for a moment, it's like something stabbed her in the heart. But she doesn't back off, just carries on with her stroking and kissing and now more French: '*Oui, ma Duchesse, oui, oui. Mais tu sais que tu ne comprends rien. Je suis la seule qui est là pour toi . . .*'

'Oh for Christ's sake!' says Wallis, trying to push the companion away.

But she's too weak to push her away and now the man-woman is furious. 'Don't say that!' she snaps. Then grabs Wallis's hand and slaps it. A nasty little stinging slap, like you might give to a dog. 'Or I'll take the pan away and you can lie in a wet bed. Do you want to lie in a wet bed?'

Kissing her one minute, hitting her the next. A person out of a nightmare. There's no talking to such a creature. Wallis can say words today, but why should she? Why should she waste her precious breath talking to this hag?

She turns her face away. Sees the girl in the apron staring at her with such a sad pitying look, it makes her weep. Fuck all these people. Piss in the damned pan and be done with them. Have them draw the curtains again. Go back to darkness.

She empties her bladder. Tells them she's done. Between them, the girl and the companion lift her again and the companion, not the girl, presses a tissue between her legs to wipe her. Kisses her cheek as she does this, fuck her. Who is she to take such liberties?

Yet she remembers this, suddenly: the touch of a girl.

God, so long ago.

When?

Lying under stars. A coal brazier to warm them. Somehow exquisite, the burning brazier and the icy sky.

In China. With Katherine. Katherine who died. Her beautiful friend, Kitty.

Kissing each other, mouth on mouth, on a silken bed on the ground. Or was it something she dreamed? Was it something she wanted to do and never did? God knows.


The room is filled with light as Wallis tries to eat some breakfast: melba toast with butter, lemon tea, a slice of white peach. At least food like this still arrives in front of her, served on bone china so fine you can see light through it. The tea strainer is still silver. Imprinted on the butter is a pattern of acorns and leaves. The kitchen has taken trouble. But she feels she should be sharing her meal with someone. Sharing it with whom? All she can remember is the feel of an eager mouth, eating from her hand.

*From her hand?*

She knows her brain's gotten all twisted up. That's what they mean by *gaga*. It's like a fog came down. She can recall the Great Fog in London in 1934 or 1935: men walking in front of buses, waving red flags; people coughing and dying; dirt on the wainscot. She can remember staring at the fog out of the window of her pale-green drawing room at Bryanston Court, and thinking how far she'd come from Preston Street, Baltimore, and how here in London she'd at last preside over a 'dazzling table'. She can remember buying candles in Harrods, glassware in Goodes. She can remember the butcher's boy, arriving on his bicycle, with the choice cuts she'd ordered on the telephone. And she can remember her husband, her second husband, Ernest Simpson. The way he always looked too big and wide for his suits. The nice habit he had of draping his heavy arm round her thin shoulders, to warm her, to keep her safe. The smell of his pipe. His man's laugh, throaty and loud. She can remember dancing with Ernest in some smart club or other. 'Isn't this just grand, what?' A striped taffeta dress. Champagne in shallow glasses. Air thick with smoke. *Tea for Two*.

But was he still there that day when she was looking out at the fog? Because, after that day, she's honestly got no memory of him any more. Did he die? Is there a grave in England she should visit? If so, somebody should darn well tell her. Ernest Simpson was a nice man.

Her breakfast tray's taken away and Wallis lies there and stares at her room. The furniture looks familiar, though she couldn't say from where. It just looks as if it could belong to her. Someone has arranged lilies in a tall vase. The silk drapes (Ernest always called them 'curtains') are a restful blue, the kind of colour she might have chosen. On the dressing table is a collection of perfume bottles – or what Ernest said should be called 'scent bottles', because perfume was a 'common' word. Ernest was helpful like this. He taught his American wife a lot about England and its little rigid ways. But these bottles look empty, as though the 'scent' in them went stale and was tipped down the john. Or else it was used up. Who knows?

Wallis turns her head and sees, on her night table, a large photograph in a silver frame. It's a picture of a young man. Who's put it there and why? Because for heaven's sake, the poor boy in the picture appears perfectly miserable! And this makes her smile, and really it *is* quite amusing how woebegone he seems. He can't be more than twenty-three. Youth should be a golden time. The boy in the photograph has some golden features, smooth skin, pale hair, ears snug to his head, but the anguish in his eyes! Heavens-to-betsy (as old Baltimore people used to say) what a world-weary look. It could make a girl depressed, when she'd got over laughing.

The companion comes in again. She always comes in, uninvited, without knocking, like she was once a butler.

'Who's this?' Wallis asks her, pointing at the photograph.

The companion purses her lips, says: 'Wallisse, you know that I refuse to answer such a stupid question. And I am getting very tired with your games.'

Games? Oh, if only there were games to play. Wouldn't that be wonderful? English country house games like hide-and-seek and croquet and sardines. Beautiful, terrifying, American games like poker. Mad, disreputable games in the evening, with borrowed wigs and men's clothes and a feeling of wanting to kiss people or bite their noses, or tell them you loved them. You could never get enough of games. They made life bearable. Now, there's no one left to play.

'You see this?' asks the companion, opening a large leather box. 'You remember what this is?'

'Yes,' says Wallis. Because she does, she remembers the smell of it, that leather smell. But she has no idea what's inside.

'So,' says the companion, 'I 'ave not let you look at these objects for a little while, because the last time I showed them you were very naughty. Very, very naughty, Wallisse. But I think today is a good day. *N'est-ce pas?* I think today you are going to be sensible and tell me exactly what they are.'

OK, so the hag's gotten her intrigued for once.

'It better be good,' says Wallis.

'It is good,' says the companion, but where Wallis looks for a smile, there is none.

She opens the box. Removes a little flat cushion. She places the box on Wallis's lap. The weight of it's more painful than a meal tray.

Wallis peers into it. Laid out on pale chamois is a quantity of jewellery. In the morning light of the room she can see diamonds shining.

'*Voilà,*' says the companion. '*Voilà, ma Duchesse.*'

Wallis's eyesight can't cope with intricate things any more. She could see the acorns on the butter – probably because, if you know something's there, you can see it better. But all these stones, these shapes blur into a snow-blind mass. Where are her spectacles?

'*Et bien?*' says the companion.

To please the woman-man, not wanting to get her wrist slapped, Wallis nods, as though to say she understands why she's being shown all this, understands what's expected of her. But she can't see the darn stuff properly. What can she do, if she can't get anything in focus?

She feels her wrist being lifted, this marmoset's little limb, and then round the wrist is placed a heavy bracelet made up of . . . what? A glint of red. A sparkle of ice. Diamonds and rubies.

'Now,' says the companion. 'This you remember. I know you do.'

Rubies bright as blood, but staunched and contained, the blood kept from spilling by the hard bandage of diamonds. There's something beautiful about the arrangement of this, Wallis admits. She didn't see it a moment ago, but oh boy, there is. This one piece, taken out of the box, released from being with the rest, is a fabulous thing.

The companion's smiling approvingly. 'Ah, I see it in your face,' she says. 'It's come back to you, hasn't it?'

With her other hand, Wallis touches the bracelet, runs her finger round it, touch helping vision. She sees it bright and clear: the rubies crammed together in square clusters, ten or more to each cluster. The square-cut diamonds separating them and yet locking them in . . .

She's lost in it. She's AWOL in the bracelet.

Who made it? Whose mind saw this lovely symmetry? Shame you couldn't crunch it, munch it, grind your teeth on it till they ached, take its essence into you, get its mineral power into your lungs, into your liver, let it break up all the old sad flesh and clothe it with new.

She'd like to be left alone with these gems. Her teeth are brittle and not all her own, yet she'd still like to bite on this bracelet like a dog bites on a bone, like a baby bites on a teething ring. She wants to ask the interfering hag to leave, but words have gotten jumbled again, she can sense this. Nothing will come out right.

'Very well,' coos the hag. 'Now tell me what is inscribed on the clasp of this bracelet.'

Another of her tests. Another of her ways to spoil any fleeting moment of pleasure.

Wallis refuses to let a syllable of anything in any language come from her mouth. She lies down with her head on the pillow, cradling the bracelet. The jewel box falls on to the floor.

'*Wallisse! Mon dieu!*'

She'll probably be slapped now, but she doesn't care. She's got the bracelet.

'Wallisse! Talk to me. Don't pretend any more. Pretence is *so* ungrateful! He gave up an Empire for you. An Empire! And you pretend to remember nothing. But I 'ave sworn to myself I shall not rest, I shall not return to my legal practice nor go again into the world until you admit to me that you *do* remember. For, somewhere in you, you do. So now tell me please: there are two words inscribed on the bracelet and you will say what they are or I am going to 'ave to punish you. I am going to punish you very badly.'

The bracelet's pressed against Wallis's mouth. Who cares what words are inscribed on the fucking bracelet? It's the thing itself that's lovely, not the words. She lives in darkness most of the time, a ghost trapped in an old TV, but now the companion's given her something beautiful and she's damn well going to hang on to it.

But the hag won't leave her alone. There's murder in her voice.

'I never thought you would be so obstinate. You are a *mule*! I dare not tell anybody what a crime you are committing. I'm too ashamed.'

Ashamed.

Wallis knows what this word means. The shame of things. Being told by her mother: 'Bessie, I can't afford that school uniform, darlin'. But, see, I'm handy with the sewing machine. Make you one so good, nobody will tell the difference.' Except she always knew. Knew it was different. There was no store label in it. The pleats didn't fall perfectly right. The shame of those imperfect pleats.

'Two words!' says the murdering hag. 'Now tell me what they are!'

Two words. What could they possibly be? Didn't romantic people make a saga about *three* words? *I love you.* If you could claim that 'I' is a word. Because it doesn't really feel like a word. More like a spool of film, whirring in darkness, snapping, breaking, spliced together again, whirring, flickering, showing you some scene or other, some far-off snow-flecked scene, only to break again, or else the projector breaks, just as you are beginning to recognise somebody or other, some castle in Germany, for instance, or that room in Baltimore where the school uniform was made, a drab room where Uncle Sol came and sometimes gave money to Alice Warfield, née Montague, sums of money that were never enough, never the same amount twice in a row, never something on which you could depend. The shame of that.

Two words.

Boarding House.

That's how they referred to it later, the place where she and her mother had to live after they left Preston Street. But 'Boarding House' was a lie, a shameful lie. It was an Apartment House. Sets of rooms, not expensive, never dusted, but like proper apartments, let to tenants. Not a *Boarding House*. A place where they could be, the two of them, separate from Grandma Anna, with her black dresses and her keys to all the closets and her ancestral furniture that creaked in the dark. And then Mother came

up with this swell idea: cook meals for the other tenants.
Turn them into paying guests. Live off that. It was a fine
scheme. And she'd do it right. She was a Montague. She
knew what people liked to eat: prime rib, soft-shell crabs,
terrapin . . .

So she'd buy these delicacies and boy, those people
came along in dozens! Squab and crawfish. They guzzled
it. Wallis went round, helping to serve them. 'Minnehaha'
was a popular waitress. She was preparing for her dazzling
table. But those guzzlers wouldn't pay enough. They kept
arguing about the cost of the meals. And then the
tradespeople started sending round bills inked in red:
*Terms strictly thirty days. No further credit can be extended.* And
men began calling, threatening. 'What's goin' on,
Bessiewallis, dear?' asked the tenants, the guzzlers. 'Oh,
nothing, Miss Brightwell, nothing Mister Carpenter. Just
some ole friends of the family . . .'

But it had to end. Alice Montague wanted it to be 'the
finest dining club in Baltimore history', but she couldn't
do the sums right and so it failed and Alice didn't know
what to do now or how to pay the tradesmen. And when
she took yet more money from Uncle Sol she whispered:
'Bessiewallis, I'm so ashamed.'


Wallis has fallen asleep, clutching the bracelet. When she
wakes up, there's somebody new in the room. She can
smell a man. She may be *gaga* but she still has a nose.

He's near her, but not right by the bed, just hovering
somewhere, smoking a cigarette. He's probably waiting to
see how *gaga* she is. Now and then, she can hear him
coughing. She says out loud: 'I hope there is a convenient
ashtray.'

Now, the man comes close. His eyes look big and blue, as if he could be wearing eyeshadow. He puts a tender kiss on Wallis's head. 'Duchess,' he says, 'it's Cecil. How are you, darling?'

Cecil? Cecil who? And she wants to ask him: 'What's all this "Duchess" business? When did that begin?'

But she can't get anything out and so the man, Cecil, says: 'No need to tell me, Wally. Dying's a cunt.'

Then he sits where the companion often sits, but he seems gentle there, not ready to slap or growl. He goes on: 'I was about to say "dying's a bugger" but ah, if only it were!' He laughs and the laugh becomes a cough. The man snaps out a silk handkerchief and coughs into that. Then he wipes his lips and asks: 'Mind if I have another ciggie?'

She wants to say that thing she said about the ashtray, but no, one does not repeat oneself, it's terribly bad form, it's worse than staring. Only small minds resort to repetition.

Cecil has beautiful hands. With these, he inserts a cigarette into a long black cigarette holder and lights it. Then he sits there, perfectly suave and serene, taking in the smoke and blowing it out again. He wears something ruffled at his neck, a cravat or scarf. His jacket is white linen. She's glad he's there.

With her little claw, she holds out the beautiful bracelet to him.

'Oh, yes,' he says, in his clipped English voice. 'One of your favourites. What a girl you were for the jewels! Was it ever true about Queen Alexandra's emeralds?'

Emeralds?

Why do men have such wandering minds? You show

them rubies and diamonds, but this doesn't seem to be enough; they drag in emeralds.

Wallis taps on the clasp of the bracelet with one long fingernail. 'Words,' she says. 'Two words.'

'What are you saying, lovey?'

She taps again. 'Two words.'

The man looks baffled. He brings the bracelet near to his eyes and squints at it. 'Oh,' he says, 'some inscription. That what you want me to see? What does it say?'

'Two words.'

'I'm blind as a mole, darling. Shouldn't take photographs any more. Can't see what's in the fucking viewfinder half the fucking time. Let me get out the old lorgnette.'

Cecil lays down the cigarette in its holder on a porcelain dish. He conjures a pair of glasses from somewhere and puts them on and his blue eyes behind the glasses look violet and strange. He holds the bracelet close to the glasses, then away.

'The light's bloody bad in here, Duchess.'

She waits. She trusts this man, this Cecil, even though he calls her 'Duchess'. He'll tell her what the two words are and then she can rest. Then the hag won't take the bracelet away.

She waits a long time. There's an evening kind of sky at the window, indigo blue, that old blue of the cocktail hour. The cigarette in the porcelain dish has burned away.

'Hold tight,' announces Cecil.

She thinks he means 'wait for it, hold on, now there's going to be a surprise'. So she keeps waiting, looking at the sky, remembering how she taught Ernest to make a good martini, saying to him: 'Nobody in England understands what to do between tea and dinner. So we're going to show them.'

'That's what it says.'

'What?'

'Your two words, ducky. "Hold tight". And then the date: "27th March 1936".'

Hold tight.

It's what they used to say on London buses. Going down Piccadilly towards Knightsbridge on a 19 or a 22. *Hold tight.* Pleased with her purchases from Fortnum's. A pound of smoked salmon. A jar of peaches in brandy. For a little supper with Ernest, just the two of them, in their new flat. Money at last. Chairs in their dining room upholstered in white leather. A silver cigar cutter from Asprey's at Ernest's elbow. His conversation so polite as he sipped the martini. His manners so British and perfect as he ate the smoked salmon. His eyes so gentle with appreciation.

Hold tight.

'It's what they used to say on the buses.'

The man in the room explodes with laughter. 'On the *buses*! Sweetheart, he never went on a bus in his life! What a card you are.'

'"Move along inside".'

'Oh, you make me die!'

The man coughs and coughs, and then he's gone. There and choking one minute, gone the next. Like her poor father, Teackle, vanished before he could be properly known, before he could be a husband or a father, leaving Alice Montague and her daughter to the mercy of Uncle Sol.

And Wallis hides by the door of their apartment, the

one where Mother used to serve up her turtle soup, her crowns of lamb, and watches as Sol puts his big, moist hands on Alice's waist. 'Won't you hold me, Alice? I do so much for you. You never show me the least . . . Without me, you and Minnehaha . . . where would you be, baby?'

Wallis knows this can't be right, Sol's rubbery mouth on Alice's neck, his hands staining the silk dress she mends in the small hours of the Baltimore morning. How could this ever be right?

'Leave my mother alone. Go away, Uncle Sol '

He goes. He crawls away down the stairs, wearing his black coat with the astrakhan collar, and they lock the door on him. They say: 'Never again. Never ever again.'

But he never forgot.

The hag would have been proud of such a man, who remembered and remembered, right until death, beyond death, into the bureaucracy of death, into the Will which states that all his money, his Warfield fortune, all five million dollars of it shall be used to set up a home for Indigent Gentlewomen.

'Indigent Gentlewomen'. Oh, you could laugh at that! You could imagine them, those indigent gentlewomen in their new 'Home', throwing away their gentility at the poker table, on the nightly drinking spree, in clouds of tobacco smoke, in secret orders from lingerie catalogues, in the way they ambush the janitor, the gardeners, the doctor who comes to tend to their indigestion and their bunions. You could make up stories about them, laugh till you wept, if only it weren't so desperate a thing, to be a Warfield and to have nothing and for the Indigent Gentlewomen to have it all.

Five million bucks.

Just to *think* of that sum. To think of it back then when it could have bought the world. To think of it and have none of it. Not a dime.

The companion's back. They're going through the ritual with the pan again except that this kind of business hurts like hell and stinks like the dead. Tears burn Wallis's cheeks. If only food could melt away inside you and not have to come out again.

'*Oh mon dieu, chérie. Quelle odeur . . .*'

In future, she'll refuse to eat anything solid. Getting rid of it again's too much of an agony.

The hag wipes her ass. No kissing this time, thank God.

The girl rolls her over very gently, with cool soft hands, and places a clean sheet under her. Soon, everything will smell of roses, of lilies, of candy, of peppermint sorbet, of forget-me-nots.

In her hand is a silver mug. 'Drink,' says the hag. A strange and bitter taste. Cold as ice and yet hot in the gut.

And it takes away pain. This and the bracelet. These are the only things she needs to remain alive; the things which fortify her blood. She knows best. It's *her* blood. Surely someone should pay attention? But oh no, the mug's taken away, the drink is finished and gone and now the companion, the man-woman, is setting her another test. Every day, there's one of these – or more. Every day, she fails them and her hand gets slapped. Or her cheek. Sometimes, the hag slaps her cheek! As though she were a kid again, stealing the good-luck charms out of Mother's ugly wedding cake, when she married for the second time; crying with rage when her favourite paper ball gown of her darling paper Mrs Vanderbilt was chucked on to the fire.

'Look at this picture, Wallisse. Here are your glasses. Put them on and look closely and tell me who this is.'

So tired. Tired of tests and puzzles. Tired of being slapped.

She can barely focus her eyes, even through the spectacles. But she tries to see who's in the photograph. And OK, it's swimming into her field of vision now, like a developing picture: a big, ridiculous hat; a fluffy veil; a smug smile; eyes too small; breasts too big. She knows who this is. Of course she darn well does! She'd know her anywhere. It's a photograph of her Enemy.

'Cookie,' she announces.

'*Non,*' says the hag. '*Non, non.*'

It's unfair to be contradicted. This is one test she couldn't fail. A girl can always recognise her Enemy, even when she's *gaga*, even when she's half blind, even when so many things have gotten lost in the London smogs.

'Cookie,' she says again.

'Wallisse. Look again. Not this "cookie". Who?'

It's Cookie all right. With her 'sweet-as-peachy-pie' smile, her fat little hands, her pearls and her dimples. There was never any mistaking Cookie. Because the one you hate and who hates you never dies or fades from your mind.

Except . . . Why was Cookie the Enemy?

Well, you can temporarily mislay the *reason* for a quarrel. This happens all the time. Or else, there wasn't any reason, like there was no reason for Win to shove her into the bathtub and degrade her and humiliate her. You can't pretend there's a reason for every last thing that happens in the world.

'*Allez*,' says the woman-man, with a sigh. 'I show you another picture.'

It's Cookie again, older, fatter, with more and more dents and dimples in her wide smiling face. Cookie with an arrow sticking out of her hat. A straw arrow! At least, she used to make them laugh. She'd appear in the newspapers sometimes. God knows why. But there Cookie would be, wearing some flouncy, tasteless tent of a gown, some stork's nest on her head, and they would howl with mirth. And that's when they thought up the nickname for her: 'Cookie', like a fat cook who doesn't know how to dress. They thought it up at breakfast time. Oh and it was just wonderful to be laughing so much, hurting and weeping with laughter. 'Cookie'! What a peach of a name. 'Cookie'!

The dogs – those sweet little dogs who skittered about on the polished floors – would sometimes begin barking, they laughed so hard. Laughing at Cookie was one of their favourite, *favourite* things. But wait. Whose favourite things? Not hers and Ernest's. Ernest had disappeared in the fog somewhere. Somebody else. A person with whom she once breakfasted. A dull little man, who hated sitting still.

'Well?' says the companion.

Wallis turns to her. That set mouth, that hard bone of her cheek. The bracelet's safe under her pillow, safe for now, but if the hag takes it away, what misery. So she tries with all her might to compose a proper sentence. She jabs a nail at the picture. Stabs at Cookie's wide and smiling face. 'This . . .' she says, feeling saliva begin to trickle at the corner of her mouth, 'is Cookie. That is what we called her.'

The picture's snatched away. The hag screams at her: 'Why do you think I'm keeping you alive? Why 'ave I – with my years and years of advocacy, of linguistic finesse – why 'ave I decided to devote my time to you? Why am I standing guardian at your gate? Because I refuse to let you die until you acknowledge your place in history!'

History? *History?* The old thing pronounced it perfectly, with the 'h' at the beginning. But what can she mean? What place in 'history' could a twice-married Baltimore debutante ever achieve?

Wallis wipes the saliva from the edge of her lips. 'I don't understand one single word,' she says.

'*Mon dieu*! I 'ave told you so many times, Wallisse. I am so tired of repeating it: you must become an honest witness to the past. I shall feed you through a tube in your nose. An iron heart will beat for yours. But you *will remember*! I 'ave sworn it. I 'ave sworn on my own life. The Duchess is going to bring everything back into the light!'

Oh, boy. She's a hell-hound, a fury. What's made her so mad? Did *her* mother die a terrible death at fifty-nine? Did this mother, right before dying, tell her she looked plain, that the brown dress she was wearing was all wrong, that her skin needed a facial stimulant? Some things you never forget.

The fury goes marching out, taking the picture of Cookie. Slam of the door, echo of the lock. Shame. Because looking at photographs of Cookie always cheered a girl up. Those bits of Cookie-pie which met in the middle: breast and stomach nudging one another like gourmandising friends. Those hawsers of pearls going round and round the turkey-wattled neck. That chiffon, all colours of pastel rainbows, which floated around the stumpy silhouette. And always that serene smile which seemed to say 'I'm Cookie-the-Beautiful', as though no one had ever told her she looked a fright, that people got stitches in their sides from laughing at her clothes, that, as an Enemy, she was a joke.

Yet, somehow, damn her, she was the Enemy with power. God knows how she'd got it, but she had. The little dull man, when he'd finished laughing at Cookie, would sometimes hurl the newspaper away and curse her. He could curse like a London barrow boy. Curse like Win Spencer. That fucking cow! That fat cunt! He would be trembling and have to light a cigarette, and his hands would shake as he lit it. He'd be near to weeping, say that it was all unfair, unfair, so bloody unfair! And then she, Wallis, would try to calm him down, tell him that temper tantrums did no good, stroke his pale head.

Who was he?

How long did he stay?

The dogs liked him. Those cute, dribbling pugs who used to sleep on her bed, lie on her feet under the dining-room table, they loved him too. But that sniffle-snuffle of their breathing used to worry him. He'd look up from his embroidery and stare at the pugs, like they were breaking his heart.

'It's the way they are,' she'd say.

'I know,' he'd say. 'I know.' And go back to his stitching. His knees would be covered in bits and ends of coloured wool. What a sad sight he was, doing his *gros point*. Hour on hour. A man embroidering his life away.

One day he announced: 'I'm going to do the Fort.'

And he meant, embroider a tapestry of it, to cover a cushion or a footstool. But the Fort was complicated. It was three-dimensional, unlike his flower needlework. He knew it was going to cause him difficulties.

It had been his house once, Fort Belvedere, with towers and turrets covered in ivy and battlements running round it, where rusty old canon still stood, pointing at nothing. He'd loved it. It was the place he'd loved most in the world. He'd owned other houses (hadn't he?), but this was the only one he loved. God knows why. All Wallis can remember of it is an elegant hall, with black and white flagstones on the floor, or marble even, everything black and white, except some tall chairs that were yellow, the colour of buttercups. Why did he love it so? Because of those startling colours? Or because he knew some hag, some fat cook, some miser like Uncle Sol would one day snatch it away from him? Alice Montague said, when her second husband died: 'Everything is taken away, Bessiewallis. Each and every beloved thing.'

Perhaps the little man had a good understanding of those words?

Anyway, he wanted to get the Fort back by doing this embroidery picture of it, but before he could start on the embroidery, he had to *paint* the Fort on to the canvas. He tried to copy it from an old photograph. But he wasn't happy with his painting. He crumpled it up and threw it in the fire, just like the paper ball gown of Mrs V had been thrown into the fire. He said his painting looked like a child had done it. He marched out of the house, informing her he was going to slash stinging nettles. He was almost weeping.

Slash stinging nettles? The things men dream up to do.

Now, Ernest had been happy with life on the whole. He'd never slashed a nettle, not as far as anyone knew.

He'd often say: 'Isn't this jolly? Isn't this a treat, what, Wallis?' Some men can be happy with their existence and Ernest was one of these. But the little man was never happy with anything, that's what Wallis remembers. And, for a while, it seemed to fall to her to try to *make* him happy. God knows why her. But the words of Anna Emory Warfield came back to her: 'Always do your best, Bessiewallis, to make people feel comfortable and content and not bored in your presence.' So she supposes someone knew she was schooled in trying to please. Whoever it was gave her the little man as a challenge.

But boy, he was hard work! Some of things she had to do. It's coming back to her now. Jesus Christ, he was so bored one time, he made her come with him to visit Hitler. In some high-up mountain resort. Cold as death. Not even any skiing. Birds of prey wheeling around in the sky above.

And that Hitler creature, with his slicked-down hair and his ranting voice, he was wearisome. No, he was. Wallis had been told everybody loved him, that he could save the world bla bla bla – but why in the world did the world need 'saving' when everyone in London seemed to be able to afford a cook and a chauffeur and a parlour-maid, when the likes of Uncle Sol were dead and forgotten, when Londoners were cheery, even during the fogs, when Ernest's shipping business was on the up-and-up, when you could buy spring violets for tuppence a bunch in Sloane Square? That's what no one ever explained to her properly: why such a lovely world needed a saviour. And it never did get explained – ever. Or else she's forgotten the explanation, along with everything else. Didn't they say it was something to do with

Communists? Communists? Surely they were too far away to matter? They were in Russia, weren't they? They stood in lines in the snow, far far away.

At Bryanston Court, one of the women round her dinner table said she was in love with this 'Führer', as Hitler called himself. So Wallis imagined someone tall and athletic, like Douglas Fairbanks. But honest-to-goodness, Herr Hitler turned out to be small and egotistical and rude. And yes, didn't he have the nerve to shut a door in her face? She can recall that: she and the little pale man were going in to drinks with him and there were other people there, men in uniform, and she, Wallis, was all dressed up in a taffeta gown and a fur stole, and hoping to God there might be a martini some time soon. And then bang! The door slams right in front of her nose. Could you imagine such a thing?

But Hitler did what he liked. And what he liked was bringing death.

She was far away somewhere by the time it happened, but there was darkness and death in London, that's what they told her, later on. This is coming back: being in sunshine miles away from where it was, but knowing that in places she'd loved there was horror beyond what she could ever imagine. And knowing Hitler had caused it. He was the architect of this horror. He slammed the door on her and on that beautiful past, and then things were never the same.

She never saw London again. Did she? It had been her home, her adopted home, and then it disappeared from sight. And everything in it disappeared from sight. The sooty parks. The trolley buses. The Ritz Hotel. The roof garden at Derry and Toms. The crowds outside the

Empire, Leicester Square. The milk carts. The baskets of violets for tuppence a bunch. The pale-green drawing room at Bryanston Court. Ernest.

So this is it. This must be it: the important thing the hag wants her to remember. She wants her to remember Hitler. How she let him kiss her hand. How, after he'd kissed it, he didn't save the world but took it all away. A girl should never forget a thing like this. The hag's right. It *is* immoral. She should be ashamed of herself.

So now she's got to call the hag, or the '*Maître*' as she calls herself, tell her OK – whoever you are – I did it: I remembered. I remembered the horror. And maybe I was to blame in some way, for what happened to the world when Hitler got hold of it. Was I? Is that why you slap my wrist, my cheek? Not only because I forgot, but because I was polite to Hitler in that mountain resort. Because, before he slammed the door on me, I sat with him on some precipice and admired the view? The little man was there, smiling, approving, as I praised the German scenery, and it was then that the Führer kissed my hand. And still we both smiled, the little man and me. Smiling with our sky-blue eyes. I guess he knew no better at the time and I knew no better and neither one of us imagined that after he'd kissed my hand, Hitler could make London disappear into darkness.

There's a bell hanging from a cord near Wallis's bed. When she presses the bell, someone usually appears. There's always a gap, between pressing the bell and the person arriving, as though they had to walk right across the damned Bois to get here. In days gone by, in Bryanston Court, servants used to arrive promptly, but here, in this ghostly room, she waits and waits, and sometimes the waiting goes on so long she can't remember why she rang the bell in the first place and she has to send the person away.

After a while, the man-woman arrives. She smells of rain. She hauls Wallis up in the bed, from where she's slithered down, then grabs a brush and begins that same, repetitious brushing of her hair she seems to want to do so often. It might be nice, except her hair's white now. White and brittle. Wallis has seen it on the pillow, like some old hermit had lain himself down beside her. Why bother to brush that?

'Stop,' she says.

'*Non, non*. I make you tidy, Wallisse.'

On she goes, the silver-handled brush heavy as iron. Wallis reaches up and clutches the hag's arm, which is always clothed in some moorland tweed.

'Stop,' she says again. 'I remembered.'

Now there's silence in the room. Not a tree moving outside, nor any far-away whisper of cars on the cobbled roads.

The companion puts away the brush, sits on the bed, takes Wallis's hand. '*Mon dieu*,' she whispers. '*Dieu soit loué*. Tell me, *ma chérie*. Tell me all of it.'

Wallis has to get the words right now. And not drool. Not come out with Afrikaans. She swallows. Preparing to speak.

'Tell me, my dearest,' says the companion gently. '*Je t'écoute*.'

The drama of it. The suspense. Like on those TV quiz shows where you could win sixty-four thousand dollars by naming the capital city of Paraguay.

'OK,' says Wallis calmly. 'I remember. Him.'

'*Oh oui, oh oui, ma bien aimée, ma Wallisse adorable.* Just say his name to me. Just whisper his name.'

'Hitler.'

Silence in the room again. No wind in the Bois. No ambulances travelling past. Not even the sound of rain. And it goes on and on. Nothing moves outside the window and here, on the bed, the companion sits absolutely still, rigid, a hunk of stone.

Then comes a horrible sound. The man-woman's crying. Her body heaves. This heaving's unearthly, like some demon crawled into her under the tweed. Oh, stop, Wallis wants to say. God almighty. But she can't breathe now, because the companion's fallen across her body and she's clutching her like a lover, her damp cheek pressed against hers, her lips against her mouth.

'Forget this,' she sobs. 'Never mention his name to anyone ever again. You never met Hitler, Wallisse. Forget this. *Oh ma chérie*, if you only knew what this does to me. Tell me you never went to that place . . .'

'I went,' says Wallis. 'There were vultures flying around the mountain. Hitler admired my cocktail gown . . .'

'No, no! Oh, my poor heart! Tell me you never met that man. You only dreamed it.'

'No,' says Wallis. 'I met him. I told you, he kissed my hand. I've remembered it all.'

The hag moves off Wallis's body, but breaks down afresh in a storm of weeping. Jesus Christ, what inconsistency! It defies belief. This terrifying '*Maître*' has spent weeks – or months – slapping and beating her and punishing her because she couldn't come up with his name, and now she's said it, she's said the name 'Hitler' out loud, and what happens? The woman has a fit. She's told to forget it again! Boy, oh boy. This is enough to turn a girl *gaga*. It surely is.

Wallis is alone again with night. Alone with the Nightmare that's always hovering there, behind the locked door. She can hear rain beating on the windows.

So OK, she got it wrong: it couldn't have been Hitler she was supposed to remember. But how are you meant to understand what to remember and what to try to forget? And where's the truth about your life – in the forgetting or in the remembering? Hell knows.

Wallis's thin hand scrabbles under the pillow to get the bracelet. Holding that against her cheek, against her lips, is so comforting, it's like the caress of a person you love. Actually, it's better than the caress of a person you love. Because love's so fragile. Well, it was for her. It was a mirage. It was just the shine in a puddle of oil.

She thought she loved Win Spencer, but he took that love of hers and messed on it. Not once, but over and over. Till she ran away and left him, told her mother no, I can't be the wife of someone like that. But oh, the look on Mother's face. 'For gracious sake, Bessiewallis, don't say the word "divorce" to me! There has never ever been a divorce in the Montague family, never ever been a divorce in the Warfield family. So don't you go bringing shame on us with that talk. My, my! What would your grandma say? Now you go right on back to that husband of yours and stay by him. Those vows you made, they're for life, unless one of you decides to die.'

He'd been posted to China, to old Canton. When she arrived, he was off the liquor, told her he was sorry, made a fuss of her, like he loved her after all. But when she asked: 'Where d'you go at night-time, Win?', he said: 'I'll show you where I go.' So he took her to a brothel, to a scented room where girls like children waited on soft couches, girls like flights of starlings, with their blue-black wings of hair and their twittering laughter.

They were real. She hasn't dreamed them, those laughing girls. Like she didn't dream Hitler. Win gave her to the girls. He said: 'Have a little fun, damsels. Teach her some stuff.'

So she lay down with them, two or three of them in a scarlet room, with their carmine lips and their soft little hands which touched her where nobody had ever touched her. And it was nice. 'So dark your hair, Wallie, so lovely black and heavy, like us! Now we touch you inside. Play a nice game. Put a small finger in. Play "trap the finger". You see? Lovely game, Wallie. Lovely feeling . . .'

Yeah. It *was* lovely. Nicer to be touched by those brothel girls than by any man. They may have been whores, but their breath was sweet. They whispered bad and beautiful things in her ear. She would have liked to stay with them till morning.

But Win hauled her away. 'Enough of that, for Christ's sake. You're not meant to *like it*, you perverted bitch. It's for learning to satisfy me. So satisfy me, right? Open your damned legs and let me see what you can do now.'

Messed on her love. Like he couldn't help himself, like that was all he knew how to do. So a girl had to run away from that, in the end, never mind what the family thought or said. You couldn't spend your life with an animal.

She had to take a passage from China all the way back

home seasick on a boat and yes, wait a minute, something happened on that voyage, something bad. She'd hoped to play deck quoits, flirt with the captain at dinner time, but she wasn't able to eat any dinner, wasn't able to stand, never mind play deck quoits. It wasn't just seasickness: it was pain shrieking inside her. Pain in her womb like you could never have imagined. Pain a hundred times worse than any Win had inflicted. Oh, God. Just to *think* of it is bad. She had to beg for something, for morphine, in fact, to lessen that agony, and then in her drugged dreams, she tried to ask the ship's doctor, what the hell is pain like this doing inside me? How did it get there? But he wouldn't answer the question. He told her she'd forget it. She'd get well again and forget.

So she lay in her little cabin, forgetting, afraid of the sea and afraid of the darkness, and when the pain came back, she thought her life was over, thought it was seeping away into the Pacific Ocean, and good riddance, for what had it been but a shameful, terrifying life and now she was going to close her eyes and forget it all.

Except, as fast as someone tells you to forget, there's someone else nagging you to remember. There's always some hag, some fiend who snaps: 'Sit up. Look at this. Watch this. And now get up. Walk to the door. You can do it. Come on. Don't give up. Don't give in.'

Will there never come a moment when she's allowed to die?

Days seem to be passing. Or it could be weeks.

For hours, Wallis holds the diamond and ruby bracelet against her lips.

The quietness of everything is strangely beautiful. And

the hag seems to be leaving her alone, thank God. After that Hitler storm, she went mercifully silent.

Then, one morning, before it's hardly light, Wallis wakes up and hears voices outside her window. They're near. They sound like they're in the damn garden. And there should not be the voices of strangers in the garden. It's what the garden's for – to keep strangers out. They sound like those people who used to gobble up Mother's soft-shell crabs, those tenants who gorged themselves sick and then bickered about the cost.

Wallis lies still as Minnehaha used to lie, when the tenants argued on the landing of the Baltimore Apartment House. One voice is getting louder than the others. Like some Yankee tycoon in a temper, and she's known a few of those! Just from the noise he's making, you can imagine how he might look: cashmere overcoat smeared with threads of rain; big bull neck kept ruddy and warm by some expensive scarf; black hairs in his ears; soft lips that no longer feel a thing, worn out from French-kissing.

He's yelling at the *Maître*. The others join in. The poor old *Maître*'s telling them all to go away, but they won't go away, of course they damn well won't. They're exactly like the tenants, or like those terrible tradespeople who never gave up with their bills and summonses: they've come to *get something*.

Wallis pushes back the bed sheets, the heavy satin quilt, tries to get her legs to move. 'When you alight from a car, Wallis, keep you knees together. Make sure your skirt is pulled well down. The world should never get a glimpse of your thigh.' So she tries to make this a dainty manoeuvre. But when she alighted from cars, there was never this pain in her stomach, this wrenching of her gut, this agony that makes a girl want to scream.

She sits on the bed, legs dangling, not reaching the floor. The damn bed's too high. She's sweating from the gut pain. The kind of pain that makes you curse or long for a morphine drip in your arm. But she's not giving up. She wants to see these people, who've gotten the nerve to approach her door. Who the hell are they? And what have they come for?

Wallis remembers there's a stick somewhere, a cane to lean on, like Uncle Sol used to do when he was old. But someone's hidden the damn stick. They thought she'd never move again, never get her wizened old ass out of the bed any more. Well, they're wrong. She's out now. She's on her pins for a moment, then she falls, kneeling, to the floor. Takes a big breath, swears at the pain, and then off she goes, on her hands and knees, crawling towards the window. What a girl! She may be *gaga*, but she can remember how to crawl.

Her long white hair hangs down. Her feet are cold, but who cares? She's always stood up to people. Always. Even her mother admired her for that. And now she's going to open the window and stand up to these strangers.

On she goes. Just like a child, except the limbs of a child are soft and bendy as a willow wand and hers are like dead sticks. She's almost at the window when she hears a new rumpus starting up outside and the Yankee yells out: 'She's dead! Isn't she? You can stop faking things, Maître Blum. We've all figured it out: Wallis Simpson is dead!'

*Dead?*

Oh, God. This had never occurred to her. She'd

thought death was still to come. But perhaps this is what death is, this room in Paris? But then why don't people tell the truth about death? If it's going to be exactly like being in Paris, why didn't somebody darn well say so?

Wallis has gotten to the window now. She raises one hand and tugs at the heavy blue drapes, and a stab of light bursts into the room, blinding and cruel. She can remember cruel light. The little man once said: 'Mama, something must be done about the light. It makes all the women look ugly.' But where was that cruel light, the one he complained about? Surely, surely, it was somewhere grand, somewhere she shouldn't have been, and weren't the King and Queen there – the old King, whatever his name was, and that upright, frightening old Queen – before the war, before Cookie was Queen-of-the-May, before London was lost . . . ?

Oh, God knows. Her thoughts are all twisted up again. The light twisted them. She must concentrate now, pull apart the curtains and get a damn good look at these strangers who believe she's dead. See if they're telling the truth or not.

But how will she know? If they say, 'Sure, you've been dead a while, Wally,' how will she be certain they're not lying? Because lies are always a part of things. Part of each and every thing. She understood that long ago. Wherever you walk, lies tread the same road. And yet he said . . . he . . . the little man . . . he said once he wanted to live his life without lying. He pleaded with her: 'Wallis, I can't lie to the world any more.' But what did she reply? Perhaps she took him by the arm or put her hand in his and told him, told him like a mother would tell an innocent boy: 'Wherever you walk, lies tread the same road.' Perhaps it was then that she first uttered these words of wisdom?

It's gone quiet outside. The hag's talking her weird French talk.

Wallis puts her cheek close to the window and peers down.

God, it looks cold there. Cold and white with snow. All the strangers are huddled under umbrellas, listening to the *Maître*. They seem good and obedient for a while, in the *Maître*'s power, just like everybody else, but then, without warning, one of them, another loud American, shouts out: 'You should be ashamed of yourself, Maître Blum! Wallis Simpson had the most breathtaking story since the Resurrection! And you've let her forget it!'

What?

Did she hear right?

Oh, boy. First it's death they're describing; now they're yelling something about resurrection. What kind of crazy stuff is getting spoken on this snowy morning?

Wallis decides she'd better ask them. She reaches up and tries to open her window, but windows in France are so damned tall and heavy, you can never get them to move. So she taps on the glass, with her nails, which are still long and painted red as rubies. Tap-tap-tap. Tap-tap-tap. And suddenly they turn. All the people turn, moving their umbrellas, and look up. She sees their faces, pink-cheeked in the snow. They stare at her. With their mouths hanging open. They look like they're seeing a ghost. And then they begin to move towards her. 'Wallis!' they call. 'Wallis! Wallis . . . !'

And oh, she can remember this: people calling her name. People reaching out their hands to her, trying to touch her. 'Wallis! Wallis!' It was so swell for a while for a girl from Baltimore. Better than being a deb at the Bachelors' Cotillion. Better than being a bride with orange blossom in her hair. Better than presiding over a dazzling table. It was what she'd always wanted. Always. To be loved; for people to say her name with love.

But it never lasted. Did it? God knows why not. First they loved her, like Win had loved her, and reached for her with their hands, and then, for no reason she can recall, they began to insult her, started calling her a bitch, an American bitch, threw rotten eggs at her car. Their love had been so beautiful and then, one day, it turned to hate . . .

Wallis lets fall the curtains and curls up on the carpet, knees tucked into her bony chest. She sees that she's wearing a white silk nightgown with a trim of Brussels lace. She's always been careful about her clothes. She just hopes there's no unsightly stain on the *derrière*.

The calling of her name goes on and on. 'Wallis! Wallis!' It's like some familiar music, long ago faded and gone.

Wallis. Wallis. Wallis!

She likes it. She hopes they'll go on calling for ever.

And now, suddenly, there's a flicker of memory, like a candle being lit in her mind: the one who loved her name so much was the pale little man. It was he who used to say it, over and over, like the saying of it was a kind of prayer or mantra or consoling nursery rhyme. 'Wallis, my Wallis . . . Wallis, my Wallis . . .'

He said it sweetly, caressingly. He said it like no one else had ever said it. And he never got mad at her. Never called her an American bitch. He got mad at the world, but never at her. Perhaps he was the only one, out of everybody in the whole damn universe (including Ernest who just disappeared into the London smog) who loved her? Because it was he, too, wasn't it, who gave her jewels? He told her some of them should have been Cookie's but fuck that, he said, they were hers now and nobody was ever going to take them away.

And not only jewels. Yeah, it's coming back now. It was he who used to buy her caviar – as much as she liked, whenever she wanted it. And boy, how she'd loved that! She just craved it like she'd never craved any other food. She knew it was expensive, she knew that ninety-nine per cent of people in the world had never tasted it, but too bad. She was one of the one per cent. Lucky her. Lucky Bessiewallis Warfield from Baltimore.

Lying very still on the floor, with the crowd still calling outside, Wallis thinks, with a smile, that she could use a spoonful of caviar now, its texture so soft and strange. It would be the one thing she could eat. And, still smiling, she decides that really she wouldn't mind if the little man came into the room and helped her back into the bed, so that she could be comfortable as she ate it. He had such gentle hands. With these hands, more gentle than a woman's, he used to spoon caviar into her mouth. Spoon it into her mouth! What an adorable, dippy little rite! Who else ever did a thing like that? And his blue eyes used to smile into hers. Smile with such love and adoration. And then he'd ask, gently: 'Is that lovely, darling? Is that delicious for my darling?'

Darling. My darling.

She said these words, too. Didn't she? Said them to him. Said them often, and with tenderness. Sure she did.

So OK, this must be it, the thing she had to dredge up

from the darkness. When the *Maître* comes pestering her next time, this is what she'll tell her: 'I've remembered him,' she'll say. 'He was too pale to have a name. I always called him darling.'

And then the whole darn thing will be put to rest.

How It Stacks Up

She says to him: 'On your birthday, McCreedy, what d'you want to do?'

She always calls him McCreedy. You'd have thought by now, after being his wife for so long, she'd have started to call him John, but she never does. He calls her Hilda; she calls him McCreedy, like he was a stranger, like he was a footballer she'd seen on the telly.

'I don't know,' he says. 'What'll we do, then?'

'Forty-six,' she says. 'You'd better think of something.'

'Go out . . . ?' he says.

'Out where?'

The pub, he thinks, but doesn't say. With the fellas from work. Get the Guinness down. Tell some old Dublin jokes. Laugh till you can't laugh any more.

'What'd the kids like?' he says.

She lights a ciggie. Her twentieth or thirtieth that Sunday, he's stopped counting. Smoke pours out of her mouth, thick and blue. 'Never mind the kids, McCreedy,' she says. 'It's your fuckin' birthday.'

'Go back to Ireland,' he says. 'That's what I'd like. Go back there for good.'

She stubs out the ciggie. She's always changing her mind about everything, minute to minute. 'When you've got a sensible answer,' she says, 'let me know what it is.'

And she leaves him, click-clack on her worn-out heels, pats her hair, opens the kitchen door and lets it slam behind her.

McCreedy stares at the ashtray. Time she was dead, he thinks. Time the smoking killed her.

He goes out into the garden where his nine-year-old daughter, Katy, is playing on her own. Katy and the garden have something in common: they're both small and it looks like they'll never be beautiful, no matter how hard anyone tries. Because Katy resembles her dad. Short neck. Short sight. Pigeon toes. More's the pity.

Now, the two of them are in the neglected garden together, with the north London September sun quite warm on them, and McCreedy says to the daughter he tries so hard to love: 'What'll we do on my birthday, then, Katy?'

She's playing with her tarty little dolls that have tits and miniature underwear. She holds them by their shapely legs and their golden tresses wave around like flags. 'Dunno,' she says. 'What?'

He sits on a plastic garden chair and she lays her nymphos side by side in a pram. 'Cindy and Barbie are getting stung,' she whines.

'Who's stinging them, darlin'?'

'Nettles. Look. Cut 'em down, can't you?'

'Oh no,' he says, staring at where they grow so fiercely, crowding out the roses Hilda planted years ago. 'Saving those, sweetheart.'

'Why?'

'For soup. Nettle soup – to make you beautiful.'

'Will it?' she says.

'Sure it will. You wait and see.'

Later in the day, when his son Michael comes in, McCreedy stops him before he escapes up to his room. He's thirteen. On his white neck is a red mark that looks like a love bite.

'Wha' you staring at?' says Michael.

'Nothing,' says McCreedy.

'Wha', then? Wha'?'

'Your mother was wondering what we might do on me birthday. If you had any thoughts about it . . . ?'

Michael shrugs. He knows he's untouchable, invincible. He's the future. He doesn't have to give the present any attention.

'No,' he says. 'Not specially. How old are you anyway?'

'Forty-five. Or it might be a year more.'

'Which?'

'I don't remember.'

'Fuck off, Dad. Everyone remembers their fuckin' age.'

'Well, I don't. Not since I left Ireland. I used to always know it then, but that's long ago.'

'Ask Mum, then. She'll know.'

And Michael goes on up the stairs, scuffing the carpet with the bulbous, smelly trainers he wears. No thoughts. No ideas. Not specially.

Again, McCreedy is alone.

But they have to do something. Like Christmas, a birthday is *there*: an obstacle in the road you can't quite squeeze round.

So McCreedy goes to see his friend Spiro, who runs a little restaurant two streets away, and tells him they'll come early Saturday evening, about seven so Katy won't get too tired, and can Spiro do steak or cutlets because Hilda won't eat any Greek stews or fish.

'No problem, John,' says Spiro. 'And we make you a cake?'

'No,' says McCreedy. 'No bloody cake. Just do some nice meat.'

Then Spiro takes down a bottle and pours two thimbles of brandy for himself and McCreedy. It's five in the afternoon and they're alone in the place, sitting on stools under the fishing nets that drape the ceiling.

'Commiserations,' says Spiro.

'Ta,' says McCreedy.

They drink and Spiro pours them another. He's a good man, thinks McCreedy. Far from home, like me, but making a go of it. Not complaining. And he does lovely chips.

He tells Hilda it's all booked and arranged, she can take it off her mind, and she looks pleased for once. 'All right,' she says, 'good. But don't go and spoil it by going out first and gettin' sloshed, will yer?'

'Why would I?' says McCreedy.

And he wouldn't have, he thinks later, honest to God, if only the presents had been better. But Hilda has no imagination. Where her imagination should be, there's an old tea stain.

Socks, they gave him. A 'Mr Grumpy' T-shirt. Tobacco. Katy draws a house in felt tip, folds it in half like a card, forgets to write anything in it.

He has to tell someone how pathetic this seems to him, how the T-shirt is grounds for divorce, isn't it?

'Absolutely,' say his mates in the pub. 'Fuckin' socks as well. Socks is grounds.'

They've done the pub up. It feels almost like you're drinking somewhere classy, except it's the same landlord with his face like a dough ball, and the same drinkers, mostly Irish, McCreedy's known for fifteen years. And they all, after a couple of pints, start to feel comfortable and full of friendliness, and the world outside goes still and quiet. And McCreedy loves this feeling of the quiet outside and the laughter within. It reminds him of something he once had and knows he's lost. It's the best.

He wants to prolong it. Just let everything unwind nice and slowly here. But he tells his mates: 'Kick me out at seven. Make sure I'm gone.'

And they promise. In between drinks, they say: 'Plenty of time yet, John, hours of time.' And the pub fills up and starts to get its Saturday night roar. And a spike-haired girl he's seen before comes up to him for a light and stays by him and he buys her a lager. She smells of leather and her skin's creamy-white and she tells him she went to Ireland once and got bitten by a horse. And she shows him the scar of the bite on her shoulder and he touches it and thinks, she's what I'd like for my birthday. I'd like to lie down with this girl and feel the spikes of her hair touch my body.

He's only twenty minutes late at the restaurant. You'd think it was two hours from the look on Hilda's face, and when he says he's sorry, she turns her head away, like she can't bear the sight nor smell nor sound of him.

'Well,' he says, 'did you order?'

'Nettle soup,' says Katy, who's wearing a funny little velvet hat. 'I want nettle soup.'

'Fuck off, Katy,' says Michael.

'That's enough, Michael,' Hilda snaps.

She's ordered a gin and tonic. She's billowing smoke out into the room. The menus sit in a pile, pushed aside, like she thinks she isn't going to understand a single thing in them.

McCreedy takes one and opens it. *Dolmades. Keftedes. Horiatiki.* Even the lettering's weird.

'Hey!' he calls, tilting his chair backwards and feeling himself almost fall. 'Spiro!'

But Spiro's in the kitchen, as he should have remembered, and it's Elena, Spiro's wife, with her mournful face, who comes over with the order pad. McCreedy tells her, listen, none of this foreign-sounding stuff, just meat, steak or chops, with chips, OK, and a pint of Guinness and Coke or something for the kids.

'Lilt,' says Michael.

'Lilt, then, for him,' says McCreedy.

'Which you want?' says Elena.

'One Lilt. One Coke for Katy.'

'Which you want, steak, pork chops, pork kebab?'

'Not pork, do you, Hilda?'

'Steak.'

'Steak for her. And for me. You want steak, Michael?'

'Yeh.'

'Katy, love?'

'You said nettle soup would—'

'Not now. Pork or steak?'

She hides under the sad little hat. It's like she's got no neck at all. And now she's going to start crying.

'It's OK,' says McCreedy. 'She'll have steak. Small portion. With chips.'

'How you want them – rare, medium, well done?'

'Well done,' says Hilda and passes Elena the rest of the menus, like she wants them out of her sight. Then she hands Katy a red paper napkin and the child holds it round her mouth like a gag and her tears are just enough to moisten its edge. She glares at her father over the top of the napkin.

McCreedy can't eat the food. It's a good steak, large and juicy. But he can't get it down.

It's partly the drink he's had, but it's something else as well. It's what his life looks like across this table. Hatred. Indifference. Love. All three staring him in the eye, waiting for him to respond, to act, to assert himself, to *be*. And he can't. Not any more. For a long time, he could and did. He fought them and held them close. He wept and screamed and tried to think of all the appropriate words of apology and affection. Right up to yesterday. But that's it, over now. They can't see it yet but he knows it's happened: they've used him up. McCreedy's used up.

He sits in silence while they eat and talk. Katy stares at him under her hat, stuffing chips, one by one. Hilda and Michael blather about Arsenal. Michael snatches Katy's steak and gobbles it down. Hilda sucks the lemon from her gin glass. All McCreedy is doing is waiting for them to finish.

And when they have, he begins gathering up the plates. Dinner plates, knives and forks, side plates, veg dishes. One by one, he piles them into a stack in front of him. It's a neat stack, like Hilda makes at home, with his own uneaten piece of meat transferred to the top plate, and then he sits back and stares at it.

'McCreedy,' says Hilda. 'This is a restaurant.'

'I know it's a restaurant,' he says.

Michael is falling around, giggling, scarlet. 'Dad,' he splutters, 'wha' the fuck are you doing?'

'What does it look like?'

'Pass the plates around again,' snarls Hilda. 'You'll make us a laughing stock.'

'No,' he says. 'There's nothing on them. Except on mine. Why d'you want them?'

'Jesus Christ!' says Hilda. 'Give us back the plates before that woman comes.'

'No,' he says again. Then he picks up his flab of steak in his fingers and lets it dangle above the stack. He takes a breath.

'See this?' he says. 'This is John McCreedy, aged forty-six today. See it? Chewed and left. Stranded. And this is all your stuff, underneath. Cold and hard and messed up. And I'm telling anyone who wants to listen that I want to get down from here, but I don't for the life of me know how.'

They all three stare at him. They don't know what on earth to make of it, except it frightens them, it's so dramatic and Irish and odd. Hilda opens her mouth to say it must be the Guinness talking, but no words come out. She begins scrabbling in her bag for a new pack of cigarettes. Michael swears under his breath and gets up and slouches off to the toilet. Katy puts her thumb in her mouth. She watches her father drop the meat and she knows what's going to happen next: McCreedy is going to sweep the stack on to the floor, where it will break into a thousand pieces.

But then Spiro is there at the table. He's smiling. He smells of his charcoal fire and his face is pink and gleaming. And he laughs good-naturedly at the stack and slaps McCreedy's thin shoulder blades, then snaps his fingers for a waitress to take the pile of plates and dishes away.

He waits until it's safely gone, and then he says: 'OK. Serious business now. Some champagne on the house for my old friend, John McCreedy. And a beautiful dessert for the princess in the hat.'

# The Beauty of the Dawn Shift

*When the Berlin Wall came down in November 1989, Hector S. was deprived of his job. He had been one of the armed Border Guards on the Eastern side, responsible for ensuring that no East German citizen crossed the wall and escaped to the West. In the course of seven years of duty, Hector S. had shot and killed five people. This is his story . . . .*

When Hector S. set out on his journey to Russia, he was wearing his uniform.

It was his winter uniform, made of woollen serge, because this was December in East Berlin. While packing his knapsack, Hector S. had told himself that he would have to travel in his uniform, that he had no choice; he didn't possess any other really warm clothes and where he was going, it would be as cold as death.

He was a man with a narrow frame, not tall, with pale anxious eyes. Women thought him beautiful, but found him frigid. He was twenty-eight and he'd only slept with one girl. This one girl was his sister, Ute.

Ute kept a pet swan in a lean-to hutch on the apartment estate. She'd named it Karl and fed it on sunflower seeds.

Morning and evening, she'd let it out to peck the grass and it allowed her to stroke its neck. There were no ponds or rivers in Prenzlauer Berg, the suburb of East Berlin where they lived, and when Hector informed Ute that he was leaving for Russia, she asked him to take her and Karl with him. But he told her firmly that this was impossible, that he had to go alone with almost nothing, just his bicycle and a bag of tinned food and his rifle. He told her he couldn't travel that vast distance – right across Poland, where he knew that hatred of all Germans, West or East, still endured – in the company of a swan.

Ute took this badly. She clutched at Hector's arm. She was already imagining the beautiful Russian lake where Karl would remember the lost art of swimming.

'Hecti,' she said, 'don't leave us behind!'

Hector S. disliked emotional scenes. When their mother, Elvira, had died in 1980 Hector had basked in the wonderful quiet that descended suddenly upon the apartment. Now, he told Ute that it was different for her, that she would be able to fit into the new Germany and that she had nothing to be afraid of. She began to cry in exactly the same way Elvira used to cry, grabbing two hunks of her hair and saying she hated being alive. Hector walked away from her. One part of him wanted to say: 'When I get there, Ute, I promise I will send for you' but another part of him wanted to remain as silent as the tomb, and on this occasion it was the tomb that prevailed.

Hector's father, Erich, on the other hand, didn't try to persuade his son to take him with him; neither did he try to persuade him not to leave. All he said was: 'A frog in a well says that the sky is no bigger than the mouth of the well, but now you have to become something else, Hector, and see the whole fucking sky. In the old imperial fairy tales, frogs turn into princes, eh?' And he slapped his knee.

Hector replied that he had no intention whatsoever of turning into a prince.

'So,' said Erich, 'what are going to become?'

'I don't know,' said Hector. 'Don't ask me yet.'

'All right,' said Erich, 'but remember, when you walk away from one place, you are inevitably walking towards another.'

'I know that,' said Hector. 'That's why I'm going east.'

What should Hector take with him? This question troubled him more than many others. His knapsack wasn't large. It was the bag in which he'd carried his lunch or his supper, depending on which shift of Guard Duty he'd been working. He would make more room in it by attaching his water bottle to the outside of it. Then there were the two saddlebags on his bicycle, but that was all.

He decided, eventually, to line the saddlebags with underwear and socks. Then he put in jars of dill pickles and some plastic cutlery. He tucked these in with maps of Poland and the Brandenburg Marshes. He added a compass made in Dresden and five boxes of matches. The knapsack he filled almost entirely with tinned meat, wrapped in a woollen sweater. There was room for a torch and two spare batteries, a notebook and a pen. He put in a solitary lemon, a precious possession he'd been lucky enough to find in his local grocery store, and he fondled this beautiful lemon for a long time, trying to imagine the tree on which such a perfect thing had grown. He packed no books, only a small photograph album, filled with pictures of Ute, including one of her naked, developed privately by a colleague of Hector's who had dreams of becoming a professional photographer. In the naked photograph, Ute was leaning on a stool with her back to the camera and her bottom was very pale in the bleached light of early morning. Her legs looked skinny and her soft blonde hair parted at the back and hung forward, revealing her narrow white shoulders.

Hector didn't tell Ute or Erich when he was going to leave, because he thought farewells were futile and also because he didn't really know. He had to set off before the lemon went rotten, that was all. He knew he would recognise the moment when it came – and he did. It was the morning of 9 December 1989, one month exactly after the wall had started to come down. He was alone in the apartment. He had exchanged all the money he possessed for D-Marks at the humiliating rate of 10–1. It amounted to DM143 and he laid it out on the kitchen table and looked at the blue and pink notes, then gathered them up, stuffed them into his wallet and put on his greatcoat and his hat. It was a fine morning, cold and clear. He walked to the window and looked out at the blocks of flats and the scuffed grass in between them where a few children played. He remembered being told: 'At the time of Tsar Nicolas II in Russia, the children of the poor had no toys of any kind. They invented games with knuckle bones.' And now, thought Hector, the parents of these children will save on food and light to buy their kids sophisticated toys from the West. He felt glad he had no children, nor would ever have any because his sperm count was too low. At least he wouldn't have to choose between absolute needs and infantile ones.

He was a man who had always known what was important in life and what was not. His chosen profession had been a difficult one, which many people would have found impossible, but Hector had never faltered in his dedication to it. In fact, he had enjoyed it and he knew that he'd mourn the loss of it. Since childhood, he'd admired the stern ways of his country, and he hoped to find these still prevailing in Russia.

He turned away from the window and picked up his knapsack. He looked at the room he was in, the room where the family ate and played cards and watched TV, and wondered if, when he arrived at his destination, he would think about this room and feel homesick for the black plastic chairs and the painted sideboard and the wall-mounted electric fire. He knew that memory was as uncertain in its behaviour as the sea; it could wash you ashore on any old forgotten beach; it could try to drown you in remorse. But he decided, no, it wouldn't be the apartment he would miss, only certain moments in it, certain moments at dawn, just after Erich left for work at the cement works on the Landwehr Kanal, when he walked from his own room into Ute's and got into her bed.

It's best to leave now, Hector told himself. Don't dwell on Ute.

So he walked out of the apartment without looking at anything more and went down the six flights of concrete stairs to the lobby where the post boxes had been installed. These he stared at. Neighbours passed him and said 'Good morning, Hector', and still he contemplated the metal post boxes, imagining news of his future life arriving one day inside them.

He took small roads out of Prenzlauer Berg and the streets were mainly deserted. These days, East Berliners trekked into the West to see what their few D-Marks would buy. He saw what they came back with: coloured shoelaces and luminous condoms. A lot of what they chose seemed to be a bright, fearful pink or a harsh lime green, and these objects reminded Hector of the day when he'd been stopped by a group of 'Wessies', dressed in pink and green shell suits, who had asked him the way to Alexanderplatz.

'What have you come to see?' he'd asked them, more out of habit than out of interest, and they had laughed and swigged expensive beer and said: 'Oh, we've come to the East German closing-down sale! Many bargains. Everything must go.' And it had been at this moment and not at any other that Hector S. had decided to leave his country and leave Ute and cycle to Russia. He said to himself, I'm not going only because I'm afraid – afraid of what punishments may be meted out to men like me, who have followed orders and done their duty – I'm also going because these people make me feel sick.

He joined the Leninallee and pedalled towards Lichtenberg. His back ached with the heaviness of the knapsack and the awkwardness of his rifle. Elvira was buried in the Socialists' Cemetery at Lichtenberg and it now occurred to Hector to make a small detour to look one last time at his mother's grave. He thought that he would confide to her his passion for Ute and in this way try to leave it behind. In her life, Elvira had relished confidences, licking her sensual lips . . . 'Oh, so delicious, Hecti! Tell me more!'

When he reached the cemetery, he couldn't remember where Elvira's grave was. There were so many hundreds of people buried here and he hadn't visited the place in five years. He knew he could spend hours looking for

Elvira and then it would get dark and he'd still only be on the outskirts of Berlin. This would be a stupid way to waste the first day of his long journey.

Then he found her: *Elvira S. 1931–1980.* A small polished stone. Hector parked his bicycle and took off his knapsack and rifle, flexing his shoulders. He removed his hat and stood, measuring the stone in his mind. The stone looked smaller than her. Did the state stone cutters cheat on everyone by a few centimetres? And if they did, was this a thing of importance? Probably not. There were so many hundreds of millions of dead under the earth, it was amazing there was any earth left on which to grow cabbages or build kindergarten schools.

Before he could form any thoughts or words on the subject of Ute, Hector was disturbed by movement quite near him. He turned and looked, and saw that a young man, poorly dressed, was going from grave to grave with a trowel, brazenly digging up the bulbs planted on them and putting them into a plastic carrier bag. The youth didn't seem to have noticed Hector – a figure of authority in a winter uniform – or else *had* noticed him and was now deliberately taunting him with his distasteful little crime.

'Hey!' called Hector. 'Don't do that!'

The youth looked up. A white face, blank, without expression. No fear in the eyes.

'Who are you?' he said.

'Border Police,' announced Hector.

'*Border* Police?'

'Yes.'

The youth stood up straight and laughed. 'Border Police! The border is down, or didn't anyone tell you? You mean they didn't tell you?'

'Please leave,' said Hector, 'before I have you arrested.'

The youth didn't move. He made an obscene gesture with his hand. '*You* leave!' he said. 'You fuck off out of my world!'

Hector was used to insults. Insults had been part of his life for seven years and now they troubled him no more than a few flakes of snow, say, or a shower of leaves blown across his path by the wind. Except that, under normal circumstances, he had his rifle with him and at this moment his rifle was a few feet away, leaning against a tree.

'You are stealing flowers from the dead,' said Hector.

The youth had a high-pitched laugh, the laugh of a girl. 'Ah, you think the dead planted them, do you, Border Guard? You think they stuck their bones up into the soil to make little holes for these bulbs?'

'This is a graveyard . . .' began Hector.

'It is?' said the youth. 'Oh, I thought it was a Communist rubbish dump. It contains the scum who made our lives a misery and a farce for forty years. But it's changing now, right? Every fucker in here was *wrong*! And I tell you what they're going to do with this place. They're going to bring in the bulldozers and dig up these stiffs and use them to put out Russian reactor fires and then when they've vacated it, they're going to—'

Hector walked three paces to his right and picked up his rifle. The click the youth heard was the release of the safety catch. The click stopped the flow of words and the pale face looked blank once again.

'Leave,' said Hector. 'Leave now.'

'OK, OK,' said the youth and put up his hands, one of which still held the bulb bag. The putting up of hands was a gesture which Hector had been trained to ignore when necessary. He aimed the rifle at the youth's groin.

'Hey,' said the youth, 'don't kill me! I know you bastards. Don't kill me!'

'Go then,' said Hector. 'Go.'

The youth tried to walk away backwards, keeping his eyes on Hector's gun. He stumbled over a grave and fell down, and the bag of bulbs dropped out of the hand with which he tried to save himself. Then he got to his feet and ran.

So there were no confidences shared with Elvira, nothing to make her lick her lips, or bring on one of her storms of weeping. And Ute wasn't left behind, but was carried onwards in Hector's heart.

Hector was sitting now in a café in Marzahn, the last housing estate in East Berlin, built to accommodate 160,000 people in 60,000 apartments, 2.6 humans to a unit. Beyond Marzahn were the Brandenburg Marshes and the wide open sky.

Hector had come to the café because after what happened at the cemetery, he'd started to feel chilly. He sat at a plastic table with his hands round a cup of coffee and the life of the café went on as if he weren't there. He hoped that, in Russia, people would talk to him more, in whatever language they could muster. He really didn't want these familiar small sufferings – feeling cold inside, being ignored by people in public – to go on for the rest of his life. But nor would he ever pretend to be something other than what he was. It wasn't his fault if ideologies had a finite lifespan, if his world was falling away like flesh from a bone, a little more each day. He'd been a Communist and a patriot. He wanted to stand up in this cheap Marzahn café and say: 'My name is Hector S. and, to me, the word "patriot" is not a dirty one.'

He sat in the café for a long time. He smoked four Karos. He went to the toilet and pissed and washed his face and hands in warm water. He stole a wedge of paper towels and put them into his overcoat pocket. He'd been told by a colleague that one of the marvels coming to East Germany in the near future would be toilet rolls printed with crossword puzzles.

Then he went out into the early afternoon and saw that it was later than he'd imagined and that a few lights were coming on in the tower blocks. Brought up to abhor waste, Hector admired the way East Germans used electricity. Light looked normal here. Across the wall, he'd seen it become more and more startling and chaotic. On the long night shifts, he used to stare at all the rippling and blinking neon and wonder if it could, in the end, by reason of its absolute pointlessness, create blank spots in the human brain.

Now, he was leaving all the city light behind. It would hang in the sky at his back for a while and he'd be able to turn round and see its faint glow and say, 'That's Berlin.' And then it wouldn't even be a glow and the flicker of his cycle lamp would be all that he had to see by.

He pedalled hard. The only weapon he would have against the cold was his own blood. He grew more and more hungry. On any ordinary trip, he would have stopped after two hours or so and opened one of the tins of spam. But he'd set a rule for this journey – one meal a day and only one – and he was determined not to break it. So he just cycled on and the moon came up and then the stars. To banish thoughts about Ute and her swan, he started to whistle some old tunes he'd picked up from Elvira who liked to sing to herself while she did the ironing.

Before night, Hector stopped at a village and bought bread. By torchlight, by the side of the road, he made a meal of tinned meat, bread and pickles. He wished he'd remembered to bring a plate to eat off as well as the plastic cutlery. Certain things, he thought, we take for granted so absolutely that they become invisible to us – and a dinner plate is one such thing.

He smoked a Karo and lay back on the frosty grass and looked at the stars. The exhaustion he now felt was suddenly intense. He knew he should repack the opened food, wrapping the bread carefully in its paper to keep it fresh for tomorrow. He knew also that he should search for some shelter, a shack or barn in which to sleep. But he couldn't move. He could barely lift his arm to stub out his cigarette.

So he closed his eyes. Some voice in him said, sleep, Hector. Sleep itself has warming properties. You'll be safe and everything will be safe till morning.

Hector was woken when the cold air of the night turned to mild but steady rain. There was enough light in the sky for him to see that a black slug was hanging off his tin of meat. He knew that he ought to remove the slug and return what was left of the meat to his knapsack, and that his ability to survive this journey depended upon such small acts of determination, but he felt incapable of eating meat that had been sucked at by a slug.

He saw now that he'd been lying by the side of a road

and that at his back was a wood. Going into the wood to relieve himself, he noticed that a narrow path ran between the trees, more or less parallel with the road. A red-and-yellow sign, nailed to an oak tree, said 'Fitness Path' and depicted a man in the attitude of a runner. Hector decided to follow the Fitness Path. Here, he would be protected from the rain and, for as long as the track ran roughly level with the road, he wouldn't get lost. Also, he liked the idea of coming across athletes. They were a category of people he admired: patriotic, stoical and sane. He couldn't imagine an athlete stealing bulbs from graves or doing crossword puzzles on toilet paper.

By his calculations, he had about a hundred kilometres to cycle before he reached the Polish border, and if his pace was steady, he expected to do this in two or three days. He hoped the beautiful forest would go on and on, right to the edge of his country. He took a long drink of water. Despite his short sleep, he felt revived, almost happy. Why, he thought, was I the only one of all my friends in the Border Police to go east? He imagined his old colleagues now, trying to sleep through this wet dawn, but most of them awake in fact, listening to the traffic beginning, listening to their blood beating, and none of them knowing which to worry about more – the past or the future.

Hector met no athletes. And, to his disappointment, the Fitness Path quite soon veered north and he was forced to rejoin the road or risk becoming lost. But by this time the sun was starting to glimmer through the rain clouds, making the road shine, and Hector's contentment didn't really diminish. It stemmed, he decided, from an acknowledgement of his own bravery. Bravery was the word. Most people in East Germany had their eyes turned towards the West, as if they were kids in a cinema queue and the West were the last show on earth. Only he, Hector S., had the courage and the vision to ride east towards the Russian winter, towards the wilderness.

He stopped at a public wash-house to shave and shower. Keeping clean was something he intended to do. He loved showers. He habitually masturbated under the shower, as did his father since the death of Elvira, and didn't care if anyone saw him do it. But here, the streams of hot water only soothed the ache in his back and in his calves, and he had no erection. The most significant thing that he had to deny himself on this journey was Ute. He knew that his sanity and his ability to keep his resolve depended on this. Only when he arrived at his destination, wherever that turned out to be, would he get out the photograph of Ute leaning on the stool and take her from behind, as often as he felt inclined. And if his yearning for her then – for the real Ute, with her soft hair and her cunt that tasted of the sea – became serious like an illness, he would send for her.

He left the wash-house with bright pink skin and wearing clean underwear. He went to a village café for coffee and a sweet cake and, although it was still early in the morning, there were old people dancing here, on the wooden café floor. The band consisted of an accordionist and a double bass player, and these two were also old. Hector stared around him. On they danced, partner with partner, men with women, women whose men had died or been mislaid dancing together, all smiling and proud of the way they could still move their feet. Hector now realised that he was the only young person in the café and he wondered whether he was in some old persons' club and had only been served out of deference to his uniform. He closed his eyes. The music was jaunty and light. A country where old people can dance in the morning must be a good country. And Hector imagined how this music could beckon people from their beds and that instead of lying under their feather quilts waiting to die, they would examine their dancing shoes for signs of wear, comb what remained of their hair, put on a shawl or a coat and walk down to the café, humming or whistling. Yet soon this scene would be annihilated by history. Hector opened his eyes and said quite loudly to an old woman who had sat down at the next table: 'This dance café will be closed.'

She hesitated. Had Hector just uttered an order? You could never predict what extraordinary orders were going to come out of the mouths of uniformed men. Once, she had been stopped on her way to the butcher's and told to remove her wig.

'I beg your pardon?' she said.

'Yes,' said Hector. 'It will be closed. In less than a year. This place will become a discotheque. They will play Western music here, pop and rock and rap, and nobody in this village will sleep, ever again. And nor will you old people dance.'

Hector had finished his coffee and cake. He didn't want or expect a reply. He'd said what he wanted to say and now he would just leave. The old woman stared at him as he got up and shouldered his knapsack and his rifle. The musicians watched him and the dancing couples watched him, but nobody spoke out. When Hector emerged into the street, it was raining again, a light but steady rain.

\*

Living in this way, off his meat and dill pickles, spending a little money on hot coffee and bread, and sleeping on the good German earth, Hector S. reached the Polish border.

He was perhaps forty kilometres inside Poland when he fell ill.

He fell ill from cold and exhaustion, and from something else he couldn't name. The illness came over him just outside the town of G., when he found himself in a landscape of striped hills, strip-farmed plough and fescue grass. And coming towards him on the quaint ribbon of road was a funeral procession, led by a Catholic priest, holding a mighty cross. And it was as if he – with his bicycle and his rifle – were the only living thing in a terrible old painting and the low sunlight was the varnish on that painting, yellow and sickly. His legs, so strong when his journey had begun, felt suddenly hollow, the weight of the knapsack and rifle on his back unbearable.

And he could hear singing. It was the priest and all the mourners defying the Communist authorities by intoning some Roman Catholic hymn for the dead person, and to Hector this human music was more disagreeable, even, than one of Elvira's attacks of weeping in the apartment in Prenzlauer Berg. It made his stomach heave.

He got off his bicycle and leaned his weight over the handlebars and the saddle. He wanted to get right away from the road, so that he wouldn't have to come near the mourners nor smell their fusty clothes nor hear them breathing as they sang, but the striped hills on either side of the road were quite steep – too steep, in fact, for a man who has been stricken with sickness.

It occurred to Hector in the next second that he would have to shoot the Catholic mourners down. This was his duty. He would start with the priest. But he felt a little confused by numbers: how many mourners and how many bullets? And confused by distance: optimum range for this calibre of rifle was . . . what? He once knew it by heart, just as a man knows his own name by heart. And then, he was suddenly confused by currencies and their terminology. Was 'dollar' a universal word, or was there a Polish word for 'dollar' that was not 'dollar' differently pronounced? Was a zloty a coin or was it a note? Was it a letter box? How many zlotys in a golden cross? How many letter boxes in a striped field . . . ?

Of course, Hector felt himself begin to fall, but a person falling may not reach the ground to his certain knowledge, but instead arrive somewhere else. Hector fell on to the grey tarmac of the ribbon road and the priest and the mourners, seeing a man in a foreign uniform lying in their pathway, came on steadfastly towards him.

Hector, however, is entering a different moment of time. He is reporting for duty . . .

It is summer, exquisite summer. It is dawn in East Berlin. Hector is entering the door at the base of a watchtower and he begins to climb up the concrete steps. Above him is the perfect octagonal of the tower itself, with its eight viewing windows. Every day, Hector notes and admires the simple yet solid and efficacious construction of the towers, so well designed for the task in hand, to enable the Border Guards to see everything going on beneath them. And now, once again, his heart is beating with pride, pride in the tower, pride in the duties which await him in the coming day. Up and up he goes. The steps are dark near the base, but as Hector climbs, he knows that when he enters the octagon – at that very moment – will be falling the extraordinary beauty of the dawn light, arriving from the East.

When Hector woke, it was dark. He was lying in a bed in a small room, painted brown and lit by an oil lamp. The flicker and fumes from the oil lamp eddied round on the brown ceiling. He could remember nothing.

Something cold touched his face. A dampness lay on his forehead. There was the smell of rose water.

Then a voice, very near, said in broken German: 'Are you waking, sir?'

Hector didn't recall making any reply, but the same voice decided to say next: 'I am a train driver.'

Then, the lamplit room and the train driver and the smell of rose water were removed from Hector's consciousness and he was submerged again in sleep, while the man (who was a driver of freight trains between Poznan and Warsaw) got up quietly and went to talk to his wife, Katarzyna, telling her reassuringly that the German soldier had woken up and that his fever was passing.

'Good,' said Katarzyna, 'so I hope he can leave tomorrow.'

'Well,' said the train driver, 'we shall see.'

'I don't want to "see",' said Katarzyna, who was old and afraid, and had a long memory. 'I want him out of the house tomorrow. I don't know why I had to marry a man with such a stupidly kind heart.'

'He was lying in the road, Katarzyna.'

'I don't care where he was lying.'

He is lying in Ute's bed. He knows he shouldn't be here, not yet. He'd forbidden himself to come here, but here he is all the same. Outside the apartment building, in the first light of morning, Ute's swan, Karl, is screeching in his cage. Ute is lying on top of Hector, kissing his eyes. He isn't inside her, but he can feel his erection begin against her flat stomach, and with his encircling arms he presses her closer to him, moving her body so that her breasts will rub against his chest. He whispers to her that he wants her, that he will want her for ever, that he can't help himself, that his passion for her will have no end, and she says to him sweetly, giggling, licking his ear: 'Hecti, it will end when you die . . .'

The dark room returned. A nightlight on a saucer had replaced the oil lamp and Hector could just make out the shape of a small window, shuttered with louvres, beyond which it was possible to imagine an icy, moonlit sky. Hector turned his head, looking for the train driver sitting beside him, but no one was there.

He lay very still. There was a wet patch in the bed and Hector supposed that he had pissed in it in his sleep, but wasn't particularly disconcerted, because this was a thing that had gone on happening to him long after boyhood and two doctors had told him that there was nothing to be done about it.

Then, hearing a train's mournful whistle, Hector remembered that he was in Poland. He remembered the striped fields and the procession of Catholic mourners. He sat up and looked around the room for his knapsack and rifle and, not finding them, was overcome with anguish. Weeping was for the weak, for people like Elvira, not for him. But in the Polish night, Hector wept and he didn't seem able to stop, however hard he tried.

After a while, he heard someone get up in the room next door and an old woman came and stood by him, wrapped in a shawl, with her hair in a grey plait. She stared at him for a few moments, then shook his shoulder quite roughly. 'German soldier,' she said, 'stop crying, please.'

Hector S. lay in the little room for another day and a night. Katarzyna swore at her husband and asked him: 'Have you forgotten the war? Have you forgotten the destination of those freight trains?'

'No,' he said. 'I've forgotten nothing.'

'Then why are we sheltering a German soldier in our house?'

All the train driver said was: 'I am a man. And so is he.'

While he changed Hector's sheets and fed him some of the beetroot soup that always simmered on the stove, Katarzyna went through Hector's knapsack and removed the lemon that she found there. She pressed it to her nose and inhaled its refreshing scent, which reminded her of days long gone, when she was a girl in a green meadow. Then she made herself a beautiful jug of lemon tea. She refused to share the tea with her fool of a kind-hearted husband, but only announced to him as she drank: 'This is the first gift I've ever had from a German. And the last.'

Two days later, Hector and his bicycle and his knapsack were helped into a truck and driven to Poznan station. Katarzyna scrubbed the room the German had vacated with a disinfectant so strong it made her teeth sting.

Hector S. was put into a freight car full of cauliflowers. 'I am sorry,' said the train driver, 'to put you with vegetables, sir.'

After this, there was just the dark of the freight car and the sound of all the miles and miles of the Polish heartland moving under the train. Hector lay down and covered himself with his overcoat, and was as still as a man can be on a bed of cauliflowers. His head and body ached, and it seemed to him that this ache was right in the substance of his skull and in the marrow of his bones.

His future was going wrong. Every thought that came to him, instead of being clear and precise, was clouded and difficult. It was as though thoughts were harmful chemicals, setting off explosions in his brain. The train was taking him nearer to his destination, but he began to see, with embarrassment, that it was towards the old eternal Russia of his imagination that he was travelling and that although he'd prepared quite well for his journey, he hadn't prepared at all for his arrival. When his D-Marks ran out, where and how was he to live? For a start, he spoke only a few words of the language. He knew the Russian word for 'now', but not the Russian word for 'tomorrow'. What kind of work could he find which allowed him to be totally silent?

Then a new thought came. The colour of its chemical felt white. It was a thought about silence and the new world, the world of the West, creeping east. Westerners were thieves of silence. They stole the quiet in a place and in the mind of a man, and replaced it with longing, just as they stole the mystery from a city by lighting it orange. Darkness and quiet were leaving the world. It was only a matter of time before the dawn wouldn't be the dawn any more, but some other computer-adjusted piece of time, with colours other than its own.

Hector felt pleased with this thought, not because it was an optimistic one, but because it seemed rational and not blighted by confusion, and so he said to himself that perhaps he was going all this way in search of the perfect silence. He'd imagined a wilderness, a birch grove, a lake, or at least, he'd imagined cycling or walking through this kind of landscape *on his way* to his future in Russia. But the truth was that the future had no location. He'd never got further with his own story than the lake. Now, he understood that he might never get further – ever. In all probability, the lake was his destination.

Hector sat up and tried to eat a pickled cucumber. He had no appetite for what remained of the tinned meat. He lay down again, liking the train now, soothed a bit by the train, as if the train were Elvira and Hector a child falling asleep on her lap, wrapped in her apron.

He didn't want to show his face in Warsaw. He knew he would be stared at and he couldn't abide the thought of meeting the stare of Polish women and girls.

He dreamed the place smelled of spun sugar, that there was dry rot in the old houses, that church bells kept ringing and ringing the hours, that pigeons continuously ruffled the air. He would fall ill again in such a place.

So he resorted to bribery. He offered DM10 to the train driver and asked him to put him in another freight going east to the border with Belarus or beyond.

The train driver took the money and looked at it and shook his head. 'Now from here in a freight train going east, you will die of cold, sir.'

'I'm used to the cold,' said Hector.

'Not this one. This is more cold.'

'Please,' said Hector.

So the money was paid and a second driver was found

who agreed to take him in a night train carrying medical supplies to Minsk. Katarzyna's husband then performed his last act of generosity: he gave Hector the blanket he kept in his cab. 'In the cold night,' he said, 'cover your body, German man.'

Hector missed the cauliflowers. In this second freight car, piled with boxes, every surface was hard and in whatever way he lay down, Hector's bones hurt. He tried folding the blanket in three and lying on top of it. This was more comfortable and Hector was beginning to drift towards sleep when he opened his eyes and saw in the darkness the freezing cloud of his own breath lying over him like a ghost. In time, he would have breathed all the air in the box car and the ghost would be very large and attempt to make more room for itself by entering the cavities of his body and taking away his life.

The blanket smelled of oil and it was old and worn, but there was still a little warmth in it. Hector stood up and wrapped himself round and round in it and lay down again on the boxes of pharmaceuticals. He imagined he was lying on glass syringes, as clear as ice.

The night would be so long. Poland, thought Hector, is a place where the nights have subdued the days and stolen half their territory. The bit of space left to the light is so pitiful, you just have time to cycle a few kilometres, buy some hard bread, pass a church where women kneel at open-air confessionals, hear a village band wearing hats with emperor's plumes play an ancient march, and then the dusk comes down, and it's futile to look forward to morning, because morning is so far away. It wasn't so mad, so completely foolish to imagine that here, on certain days, you could go into a post office, say, to buy a stamp, and that when you came out again with the stamp in your wallet, the day had given up hope and the words 'post office' had faded into the wall.

These thoughts made Hector remember the line of post boxes in the lobby of the apartment building in Prenzlauer Berg and how he'd imagined letters from Russia arriving there, letters which described an epic journey, an honourable arrival, a life built in a place where the structures of the old familiar world were still standing.

Now, in his freight car, wrapped in the train driver's blanket, as heavy snow started to fall, Hector began to compose in his mind a letter to Ute, to the sister he'd desired since the day, at the age of five, when she'd licked his penis in the bath. It might be, he thought, the only letter he would have time to think up, and so he wanted it to describe a place that would seduce Ute, a place in which she would recognise that she could be happy, a place he had made safe for her in advance.

*Dear Ute,*

*I have arrived at the loneliest, most beautiful place in the world. Let me describe it to you. It is a great forest that has been growing silently for more time than anything else on this part of the earth. Bears inhabit it. And reindeer and wolves. Snow lies over it for seven months of the year. Sometimes, I fall into conversation with a solitary hunter and we discuss weapons and the individual characteristics of flight of certain difficult targets and how, in one's aim, one may compensate for these and so kill after all and not starve. Bears are protected and may not be shot.*

*And this brings me to swans. At the feet of the forest is the lake. The north side of it is frozen, but a little water still laps the snow on this southern side and here I have discovered a fine family of your favourite birds. They whoop like cranes in the early morning. They're plump and sleek from the quantity of fish they find in the lake. They are as tame as Karl and will come if I call them and feed from my hand. When you join me here, this is the first thing we will do: go down to the lake and visit the swans.*

*I expect you're wondering where we're going to live and how we're to find shelter. 'Hecti,' I hear you say, 'are you asking me to make love to you in the snow?' No, Ute. No, I'm not. Unless you want to do that.*

*I have found, at the lakeside, an old grey dacha, built of wood, with a stone chimney and a steep shingled roof. I walked into it like that girl in the fairy story and sat down in the largest of chairs. I found a smoked ham hanging inside the chimney. I found a larder full of apples. I found folded sheets for the bed.*

*It's as if this dacha was designed with me in mind, with everything necessary for my survival: an axe to chop wood, a fire to cook on, even a feather-bed quilt for the nights, which are as cold as nights on the moon. So now, I'm able to say to you, don't waste any more time, sell whatever you have to sell – Elvira's hairbrushes, father's cache of cigarettes – and take the next train out of Berlin going east . . .*

It was at this point in his imaginary letter that Hector was jolted forwards and almost fell off the ledge of boxes on which he was lying. The train had stopped.

Hector listened. He hadn't seen the thick snow falling, but by the temperature in the car and by the absence of any sound, he was able to judge that it was the deep middle of the night. The train would still be a long way from Minsk, a long way even from the border, so he supposed that it must have stopped at a signal and that in a few minutes it would get going again.

Somehow, the immobilisation of the train made the cold inside the freight car more intense and the ghost of breath that filled the space around and above Hector became agitated and began a strange kind of wailing.

The train moved. But it was going backwards, Hector could tell by the way his body rolled. And then it stopped again. Hector raised his head off his knapsack, to hear better, to see better, but he could hear and see nothing except the ghost in the air.

What Hector couldn't know was that the train had been rerouted into a siding because the line further east was temporarily closed by snow. What he couldn't know either was that the driver of the second freight had forgotten all about him and, once the train was safe in its siding, got down from his cab and walked away across the white fields towards a village, in search of a warm fire and a bed for the rest of the night. So Hector lay there, waiting for the train to resume its journey, while the soft snow piled up on the roof of the box car.

After an hour had passed, he tried to move himself towards the edge of the car, so that he could bang on the doors with his feet, but he found that his body was unwilling to move. It asked him to let it rest. He attempted, then, to call out. He knew that a human voice inside a freight train would probably make the kind of sound that disturbed one's peace and altered nothing in the world, but he tried to call nevertheless. 'Train driver!' he said. 'Help me!' It was a whisper, not a shout. Hector believed that he was shouting, but he was only murmuring. And anyway, the driver of the second freight was a mile away.

He was sitting by a fire with a schoolteacher and his wife, drinking vodka and eating poppyseed cakes.

After his efforts at calling, Hector's throat felt sore and he was afflicted suddenly by a desperate, unbearable thirst. He had no memory of where his water bottle was or when he had last seen it, but what he did remember was the solitary lemon he had put into his knapsack on the morning of his departure. And his longing, now, to suck the juice from this lemon became so great that he succeeded in extracting one hand from the blanket and with this one hand reached behind his head to try to undo the fastenings of his knapsack.

He could picture with absolute precision the colour, shape and texture of the lemon, as clearly as he could picture the icy Russian lake and the grey dacha beside it, in which he and his beloved sister would live. And his yearning for the freshness of the juice of the lemon was so deep, so absolute, that into his search for the precious fruit he put every last ounce of his strength.

The snow stopped falling an hour before sunrise and the sky cleared and the dawn was bright.

Woken by the winter sunlight, the driver of the freight to Minsk remembered at this instant the German soldier he'd agreed to hide in one of his box cars in return for DM5.

He dressed hurriedly, tugging on his overcoat and his hat, and let himself out of the schoolteacher's house.

The snow was thick on the fields. The man wasn't young. Trying to make his way through this deep snow was exhausting for him and it took him the best part of half an hour to reach the train.

He opened the door of Hector's box car and stared in. The light on the snow had blinded him and, for a moment, he could see nothing. 'Hello!' he called. 'Hello! It is morning.'

Hector was lying face up, one arm behind his head that rested on his knapsack. The German's face had the pallor of bone, but there was a smile on it, as if, in his last moments, Hector had glimpsed something strangely beautiful.

The train driver walked a few paces from the car and fumbled to light a cigarette.

He stood in the snow, thinking.

It didn't take him long to decide what he was going to do. He was going to leave Hector exactly where he was. He wasn't even going to touch him or cover his face. Even if the day remained fine, the cold in the box car would preserve his body and, with a bit of luck, the train would get to Minsk before nightfall.

At the depot, the freight would be unloaded by rail workers from Belarus, and so it would be they who would find the stowaway. In this way, provided he remembered to get rid of the German currency, the driver would have shifted the burden of responsibility. The dead German, wearing some kind of military uniform, would become a Russian problem.

Death of an Advocate

*Inspired by the painting 'Holyday' by Tissot, c. 1877*

*By permission of the Tate Gallery, London*

The thing which first annoyed Albert about that afternoon was everybody pretending they weren't cold.

He considered this ridiculous: his wife, Berthe; his sister-in-law, Marianne; his parents-in-law, Claude and Joséphine, sprawled there on the tartan picnic rug in the weak October sunshine, drinking their tea, smiling, listening to the birds, as though this were a hot day in July.

'You know it's freezing,' Albert announced.

Nobody paid him any attention. They just carried on sitting still. For that was what this picnic seemed to be about: eating cake and sipping tea and then falling silent and staring at Nature – or what passed for Nature in this part of the municipal park. Everybody hunched and separate and in a reverie of his own. Albert noticed with irritation that the women even pretended the chestnut leaves weren't falling on the picnic cloth. They let them lie there, as though they didn't see them, or as though the brown leaves might have been slivers of fruitcake left half-eaten through inattention.

'Stupid,' said Albert under his breath. 'Absolutely stupid.'

A wasp arrived and began crawling over the cake. He

stared venomously at it. As a child, he'd almost died from a wasp sting. The natural world waged a senseless war with man which exasperated Albert. How he hated this kind of Sunday outing! He wished he were in his office in the rue St Hippolyte, immersed in the Estate Accounts of one of his solidly wealthy burgher clients, or, better still, about to read out – in all the glory of its repetitive and complicated language – the Will of an aristocrat to the dead man's confused and betrayed wife.

Albert loved this work. Love was not too strong a word to attach to the feelings he had for it. Berthe sometimes teased him that he loved only the fees he earned, those rounded ten per cents which followed one another in a steady and almost unbroken stream. '*Non, ma chérie*,' he always told her, 'it's the lawyer's work itself, that *sorting out and tallying up of things*, which I adore.' Albert went so far as to admit that he often felt himself to be boiling up with contentment in his chosen profession. 'Boiling up' was how he liked to put it. Because it made him hot and scarlet, and he could feel his feet burning and he could imagine his liver, beet-red and glistening.

But now, sitting in the park on this October Sunday in the year 1877, Albert felt cold. He picked up one of the voluminous table napkins provided for the picnic by Berthe and wound it round his neck. Marianne giggled. 'I don't know what you look like!' she said.

'If you don't *know* what I look like, then why did you say anything, Marianne?' said Albert. 'If you had found some witty comparison between me and, say, some little-known species of marsupial, then you might have given us a moment's amusement, but as it is you've just wasted your breath.'

Berthe, against whose familiar rump Albert was reclining, turned her head and looked sharply at him. Why, came her unspoken question, was he being so pompous and disagreeable, especially to Marianne, upon whom, everybody knew, he doted in a way that was sometimes almost troubling?

Why indeed? *Why?* Albert didn't know. He stared at Marianne, at her pretty face under her smart Sunday bonnet, at the bodice of her striped taffeta dress and waited for the pleasurable and familiar feeling of mild lust to arrive in his groin. But what arrived instead was a feeling of boredom so crushing, so absolute, that Albert had the sensation of falling over. He was glad that he wasn't standing up, for then, surely, he *would* have fallen over. It was as if the sky had literally darkened, or as if the universe were collapsing in on itself.

Albert looked away from Marianne. He saw that he was still holding his teacup. He examined his own thumb on the rim of the saucer. He thought how plump, pink and ridiculous this thumb appeared. He set the cup down and now realised that everybody had turned away from him: Marianne and Berthe and his six-year-old daughter, Delphine, and Claude and Joséphine. All of them had turned their backs on him. The child was whispering something to herself, one of her little songs, but the grown-ups remained silent and unmoving, and Albert wondered whether they knew what was happening to him, knew that his universe was faltering and that, lying as he was near the rim of the pond, they were simply waiting for the moment when he would roll backwards and fall into the water and drown under the flat green leaves of the water lilies.

Albert rubbed his eyes. Then, one by one, he examined the things that lay within his vision: the tea caddy, the teapot on its stand, some bottles of water, the half-eaten cake, the wasp, a plate of biscuits, the fallen leaves, the knives and forks, the white cloth, the edge of the rug, the grass beyond, the shadows of clouds on the gravel walkway. He expected to find consolation in one or other of these things, especially in the tea caddy, whose square shape and ivory handle he had always found aesthetically pleasing. But now, on reflection, Albert decided that a tea caddy was a ridiculous object; in itself and through-and-through an unnecessary thing, balefully ugly and superfluous to human need. He wanted to rage at the mind that had invented it.

At this moment, Delphine picked up her skipping rope and asked her grandmother if she could go and do some skipping on the gravel walkway. 'Yes,' said Joséphine, 'but go right over there, so that you don't kick up dust into our faces.'

Albert looked away from the tea caddy, over to where Delphine now stood in the sunshine, laying out the rope in front of her feet, then experimentally jumping over it, to remind herself what skipping involved. Though he was pleased to discover that these little gestures still touched his heart, Albert soon realised that what they touched his heart with was sorrow: sorrow for Delphine's loneliness in a grown-up world, sorrow for her future as the wife of some unfaithful husband, sorrow for her mortality. Though he loved her, he wished at that moment, as Delphine began to skip, that he had never brought her into the world.

He couldn't lie there any more, shivering with cold,

leaning against Berthe. Though his legs felt weak, he stood up, brushing crumbs from his jacket, and walked towards his daughter. 'Watch me, Papa!' she called out, so he did as she asked, watching the concentration on her face, and then watching her feet, shod in brown boots, jumping up and down in the dust.

He slept badly that night, for the first time in his life irritated by the smallness of the double bed, by the solidity and heat and nearness of Berthe. That afternoon, he'd been cold; now he was far too hot. He wanted to be in a narrow space of his own, in absolute darkness, with the sheet pulled taut and cold and clean across his chest. When Berthe began snoring, he wanted to bundle her out on to the floor. 'What's *happening* to me?' he asked himself.

Albert turned his back towards Berthe and lay staring at the darkness. He began counting money in his mind, which is what he often did to encourage sleep: adding up the total of all the ten per cents, actual and probable, that he would earn before the year's end. The figure he arrived at was large and encouraging, but almost immediately the thought came to him that money, these days, simply remained money. In his youth, or even until quite recently, it had always been alchemised into purchases and acquisitions. But his house and office were now stuffed with these purchases and acquisitions. Albert couldn't think of one other single thing that he wanted to buy. In fact, he decided, there were a number of things that he would like to throw away, starting with the ivory-handled tea caddy.

The logic of this was depressing. For if there was really nothing more that he wanted to buy or acquire by any means, what was the point of continuing to work as a lawyer for the next twenty or twenty-five years? A consoling (but strangely weary-sounding) voice in Albert's head reminded him that he enjoyed his work very much – for its own sake, for the satisfaction of turning chaos into order, muddle into transparency, expectation into fulfilment. What he earned was far from being the only important thing. But the next realisation to torment Albert, as the birds began their dawn revels outside his window, was that the vocation of a lawyer specialising in Estates and Wills amounted to nothing much more than the job of a *femme de chambre*, commanded to tidy out the piles of forgotten junk people kept in their attics. All he did, in the end, was move things around. (And then take away some sizeable pieces for himself.)

He became aware, at this moment, of Berthe waking up. Hearing her stir and sigh and reach out one of her plump arms for a sip of water from her bedside cup, Albert remembered how these intimate noises used to move him, and how it had often seemed like a miracle to him that this sweet-natured and beautiful Berthe was his wife. But now, he saw, as he lay pretending to sleep, that he was indifferent to her. He was tired of the smell of her hair. He didn't really care whether she lived or died.

Albert dragged himself to his office, but cancelled all his appointments with clients. The thought of talking to rich people made him feel ashamed. As the afternoon came on, he decided that he couldn't endure this town any more. It was surely the familiarity of everything in it that had brought on the unbearable sadness of his mind.

He booked himself a wagon-lit on the overnight train to

Paris and, once installed on the hard little bed, hearing the wheels of the train grinding on the shining rails, he felt his spirits lift a little. 'What I'm experiencing,' he told himself as he lay there, 'is just the onset of middle-aged pessimism. I'm forty-three and my stomach is too large for every single pair of my trousers. I'm feeling the anguish of one who's become too fat for the world he's in.'

It was thus, as Albert drifted off to sleep, that he dreamed of how, for a few days, he would change his world. He would visit Jeanne, his favourite dancer at the Moulin Rouge. He and Jeanne would drink champagne and dance to gypsy violins and make love in a noisy and indecent way. Jeanne, who had nothing, no possessions, no apartment of her own, nothing at all except her beauty and her clothes and her meagre salary from the Moulin Rouge, would console him. She would make life seem beautiful again. Because forty-three was not old; it could be the prime of his life. Perhaps, in a few years' time, he would have made enough money to move to Paris and set up a practice there. And in Paris, he decided, there would be no more picnicking and family outings. They killed a man, these things. They destroyed his curiosity and his desire.

When Albert woke, as a pale sun began to shine through the train window, he became immediately aware of an odd, tickling sensation on his mouth, as though Jeanne might have been stroking it with a feather.

He reached up to his lips and found, to his disgust, an insect crawling there. He swatted it away: a large wasp, heavy and stupid in its autumn torpor. It fell on to the red blanket which covered Albert and as he looked around for something with which to kill it, a burning pain in his mouth assailed him. The damned wasp had stung him!

Albert leaned up on his elbow. As the pain intensified, he thought how he had been lying exactly like this at the picnic in the park, but with his head resting against Berthe, and now, alone in the wagon-lit, he began to cry out to Berthe, saying her name, gasping it out as the venom from the wasp sting – the same venom that had almost killed him as a child – entered his blood and began its lethal work. His throat constricted. His lungs began to burn and ache. He doubled over in his agony, trying to reach out for his cup of water, but knowing, as his hand scrabbled to find the cup, that water wasn't going to save him.

And Albert thought that this, this death by suffocation, by asphyxiation, was exactly the death he had always feared, the worst death, and he cursed it and cursed despicable Nature which had caused it.

In torment, he hammered on the window of the wagon-lit. He tried to call out to the fields and woods and hedgerows speeding by. He tried to tell these green and indifferent things that he was too young to die. He tried to say that it was barely the autumn of his life and that on the beautiful surface of his existence, hardly any leaves had fallen.

# Nativity Story

I had a child once. A boy called Daniel. He was just learning to crawl and make noises that sounded like words when my wife left me and took Daniel with her and I never saw either of them again. My wife packed up all the baby paraphernalia and every single one of Daniel's toys and all his little clothes, so there was no evidence left that he'd ever been part of my life.

I went searching in drawers and under furniture, looking for something left behind, but there was nothing left behind. When I was drunk – which I often was – I thought, well maybe I just dreamed this little Daniel? Because I'm prone to spells of weirdness. People stare at me and say: 'Mordy, what's going on, then?' And sometimes I can't go to work. Sometimes, when I wake up, the world looks so abnormally bad that I have to cower in my room.

I'm a chef. Well, a cook. Chef's too poncy a word for what I do. But I'm good with eggs and I know what proper chips should be like.

I never stay in one place for long. It's like I'm afraid I'll look up from the fryer one day and see my ex-wife and my son eating food that I've made and be filled with a sadness I won't be able to bear. So I keep moving on. On and on.

And more and more I keep away from towns, choose places way out in the countryside: motels, guest houses and B-and-Bs. If you work in these places, especially out of season, you can often get a room in them, the smallest, cheapest room they've got, but the room's part of the deal and then at least you can sleep OK and go to work clean and smelling of shower gel. And I've got no possessions. Not as such. A few clothes, a little tobacco tin, a torch. Oh, and an oyster shell. I did a stint at an oyster bar round about the time when Daniel was born and one oyster I opened had such a fantastic pearly shine inside it that I took it home and scrubbed it and stored it away, wrapped in a rag. I thought I'd give it to Daniel when he was older. I imagined myself showing him the shiny shell and saying something pitiful like: 'There aren't that many beautiful things left in the world, mate, but this is one of them.'

When last winter began, I found a job in a big old run-down hotel that was empty most of the week but on Saturdays and Sundays hosted 'Dance-and-Dream' week-ends for elderly people. A 'Dance-and-Dream' weekend was one in which you played bingo or roulette all day and dreamed about the fortune you could win, and then in the evenings danced to a three-piece band who played rumbas and tangos and old embarrassing songs. The average age of the Dance-and-Dreamers was seventy-nine.

In the kitchen, we made steak pies and sherry trifle. The steak had to be soft and tender, and the trifle extra sweet. Late at night, just as the kitchen was closing, orders would come down for hot chocolate and malted milk.

During the week, I occupied quite a nice room with two beds in it and coffee-making facilities and a shower of my own. But the Dance-and-Dream weekends caught on so well that the bookings increased fivefold and the hotel manager had to take me aside and say: 'Mordy, you don't mind roughing it, do you, just for the two nights of the D-and-D? We'll make it up to you in tips.'

I was taken down to an enormous room in the hotel basement, which smelled damp and weird, like some breathing creature had once lived there, chomping on the green moss of the snooker table. There were big leather sofas round the walls, where the snooker players once sprawled around and smoked, and the manager said I could sleep on one of these and wash myself in the rusty little toilet the players used. It was cold down there and the floor was damp in places, but I said it would do. Since Daniel left, I can't bring myself to care that much about where I am or on what surface my body has to lie.

On the Saturday of this particular D-and-D weekend, the weather had been misty and mild, but on the Sunday, during bingo and while we were simmering the steak and opening cans of peaches for the trifle, you could feel the outside temperature suddenly drop.

I opened the pantry door and looked out on to the pitch-dark yard. An amazing frost had crept up on everything in sight, hard and glittery as sugar. I called over the other chef, whose name was Rinaldo, and we stood together breathing the frozen air and looking up at the stars, which seemed incredibly near and low, like they were crowding out of the cold universe to get some warmth from us. 'Phew, lucky our Dancy Dreamers not goin' any place in their cars!' said Rinaldo. 'Very lucky tonight.'

I got to bed on my leather sofa about one o'clock. It was really cold in the basement and my blankets were itchy and my pillow made a crunching noise every time I moved my head, like it was filled with barley husks.

I knew I wasn't going to be able to sleep. I got out my oyster shell, to see if it had kept its shine, and this staring at my shell seemed to calm me. I was just on the brink of sleep when I heard voices on the basement stairs.

The overhead light snapped on and I saw the manager at the door in his dressing gown and with him was a young couple. The girl was whimpering and being comforted by the bloke, who was pale and thin with a nerdy kind of beard. The manager was carrying an armful of blankets and pillows. 'This is it,' he said. 'This is the best I can do for you. At weekends we're absolutely chock-a-block full.' Then he said: 'Oh, Mordy, sorry. I'd forgotten you were down here. These poor people's car went off the road. They're not hurt, but they're dreadfully cold and tired. Can you help them get comfortable?'

I put my shell away. The woman stared at me in confusion. She thought she'd be shown into a proper room with a shower and a double bed with clean white sheets, and now she found herself in an old snooker den with a man who smelled of cooking oil. And I wasn't even wearing proper clothes, only a string vest and a pair of boxer shorts.

I tried to reassure the couple that I wasn't drunk or weird – just a chef who had no family. I showed them the rusty toilet and helped the guy pull two sofas together and lay out the blankets and the scratchy pillows while the girl went to wash away her tears of cold and fright. The guy's name was Joe and he had a quiet voice. In this soft little voice of his, he told me he worked as a kitchen fitter.

The girl wouldn't speak to me or look at me. She just kept her coat wrapped round her and got under the blankets and turned her face away. Joe whispered to me: 'Nothing personal, mate. She's just a bit traumatised by what happened with the car. She'll be OK in the morning. And I'm sorry we've interrupted your night.'

We put out the light and tried to go to sleep. I could hear Joe talking softly to the girl and I couldn't help thinking about the days when I'd had a wife to talk to in the middle of a freezing night. I could remember the smell of her hair and the way she breathed so silently you couldn't tell if she was alive or not.

I don't know what time it was when I woke up.

The light was on. The guy Joe was bending over the girl, who was lying on her back and gasping. There was a weird smell in the air and parts of the floor were wet.

'What the hell . . .?' I said.

Joe said: 'Sorry about this. Does the hotel have a doctor? Could you go and phone?'

'What's wrong with her?' I asked.

'Oh, nothing,' he said vaguely. 'She's just having her baby.'

'Having her *what*?' I said stupidly.

'She'll be fine,' said Joe. 'But I guess we ought to get somebody. If you could . . .'

I wrapped a blanket round me and went up to the hotel foyer, which was silent and dark. A tray of malted milk cups had been left on the reception desk. I put on a couple of lights and reached for the phone, then put it down again because I didn't know what to dial. Was I meant to call the emergency services or wake the manager, or what? When my wife was about to have Daniel, we just went calmly to the hospital in a minicab . . .

I saw a packet of fags lodged on the hotel switchboard and I took one of these and lit it and tried to decide what I was supposed to do. Memories of the birth of Daniel kept coming to me and distracting me from the here and now. I thought about the moment when the surgical mask had been tied round my face and the way my wife gripped my hand when her contractions came and how her hair got damp and stuck to her head. And then I remembered the doctor and nurses suddenly scurrying about and doing things, like there was an unexpected emergency and I said: 'What's happening? Is everything OK?' and they said, 'Yes. Everything's fine. Everything's under control.' And then Daniel came out. He was covered in blood and a sort of whitish gunge. He was wrapped in a bit of green material and laid on my wife's breast and as I bent over them, I could hear a sound coming out from behind my surgical mask and I thought, fuck, I'm crying.

I lit a second cigarette. I still hadn't telephoned any-body. When that second fag reached its end, I thought I would go and wake up the manager and let him decide what to do. I was stubbing out the ciggie when I saw one of the Dance-and-Dreamers coming down the stairs. He was an oldish guy with a bald head and a tiny little crown of fluffy hair going round it. He was wearing a dinner jacket and in his hands he was carrying one of the prizes he'd won at the bingo game. It was a useless glittery box, made out of mosaic pieces.

He nodded to me. He looked rosy-cheeked and happy. He said: 'Did you see those stars?'

And I said: 'Yes, as a matter of fact I did, sir.' And then he went on down along the corridor, heading for the basement.

I was thinking, what on earth is that old geezer doing wandering about in his dinner jacket at four in the morning, when I heard someone calling my name. It was Rinaldo. He'd appeared from out of the kitchen area, wearing his chef's whites and his chef's hat. 'Mordy,' he said, '*fantastico*! Don't you think?' Under Rinaldo's arms were two bottles of Vermouth.

'What?' I asked. 'What?' But he was gone, also heading for the basement. And I thought, God Almighty, what's going on in this bloody place? This is the weirdest night I've ever lived.

I picked up the telephone receiver again and was looking down the hotel listings for the manager's number, when I heard more footsteps on the stairs. It was the manager himself. And he was carrying the huge arrangement of sunflowers that normally stood on a table on the first floor. It was so enormous he could barely hold it or see round it, so that some of the sunflowers looked as if they were growing out of his head.

I washed the smirk off my face. I said, 'I was just about to wake you . . .'

'Yes, Mordy,' he said. 'I should think you were!'

He bumped into me as he passed and a couple of golden petals fell on to my shoulder. I put down the phone and walked behind him, talking as I went, but the manager didn't seem to be listening to me, so I just obediently followed where he led, which was back down the stairs to the basement and then into the snooker room. As we went in there, I thought, that guy Joe is going to kill me.

It was absolutely quiet in the snooker room. The girl was sitting up inside the two pushed-together sofas and in her arms was a baby, wrapped in a pillowcase. Joe, the husband, or boyfriend or whatever he was, stood behind her, with one arm round her shoulders, and both of them were smiling, like the birth had been really easy and nobody had panicked because there was no doctor and no pethidine and in fact no *nothing*. There were only the shabby sofa-bed with its barley-husk pillows and a single overhead light.

And then I saw that the Dance-and-Dreamer was on his knees on the dusty floor, offering up his bingo box to the couple and their baby. He didn't seem to be minding about the dirt on his dinner jacket nor about the creak in his old knees. He looked flushed with happiness.

Rinaldo was kneeling, too. He'd put the bottles of Vermouth on the sofa and I saw him reach out to the baby in the pillowcase and lay his hands on it tenderly, just like he'd lay his hands on his pizza dough before he began to shape it. And there was something about all this that made me feel shivery and strange. I wrapped my blanket round me and went to my sofa and sat down.

Soon after that, more people started arriving in the snooker room. I lost count of them, but I think that just about every one of the Dance-and-Dreamers came tottering in – some dressed in their dancing finery, some just in their night clothes, two couples with their dogs which normally whimpered and yapped but which were quiet as could be – all bringing stuff for the couple and their child, and laying these things all around them so that the sofa-bed disappeared under a mound of peculiar presents: washbags, clothes brushes, bed jackets, bars of hotel soap, shoe-cleaning kit, paperback novels, half-finished knitting, satin coat-hangers and tins of Complan.

After a long time, I opened my mouth to say: 'Will someone please tell me what is going on?' But these words didn't come out. Nothing came out. I wasn't capable of speech. Because what I felt inside was a horrible feeling of loneliness and misery. I was the only person in that massively crowded room who had no gift. I was apart from everyone, wrapped in my blanket, all alone in my corner, while everybody else was in a happy sort of hugging-and-kissing mood, and the bottles of Vermouth were being opened and passed around. I thought, there's a party going on – a surprise party – and I'm missing it, just like I seemed to have missed out on all the important things in life.

Then I remembered my oyster shell. I'd sworn I'd never part with it. It had been intended for my son Daniel and no one else. But now I got it out and polished it up. I wormed my way through the big throng of people. I laid the shell down on the girl's pillow, and I saw everyone nod approvingly and the girl swivelled her head and looked up at me. And her face softened into a fantastic smile. The happiness and relief I experienced when that smile came were huge. And I felt Joe's hand laid gently on my shoulder. 'Grab a tot of Vermouth, Mordy,' he said and held out the shining bottle.

# The Over-Ride

When Stefan Moutier was a child, he was forbidden by his mother to sit on the stairs.

Madame Moutier was the concierge of an expensive building in the 8th Arrondissement of Paris and she would remind her son: 'The stairs are not ours. They are the residents' territory and you shouldn't be there.'

But Stefan had noticed other things on the stairs which looked as if they shouldn't have been there: cats sleeping; bags of garbage left out. And so he disobeyed his mother. He decided to become as silent as a cat, as shapeless as a bag of garbage. That way, the residents would walk right by him and not notice him.

The most famous residents of the building were Guido and Claudette Albi. Madame Moutier boasted about them to the concierges of other buildings in the area: 'The Albis, you know, the world-famous musicians.'

But these other concierges often said: 'Yes, Madame Moutier. But beware. Artists are trouble. In the end, trouble will come.'

But trouble did not come for a long time. What came, all through Stefan Moutier's childhood and adolescence, was music. And this was why he sat crouched on the stairs. He was listening to the tides of Mozart and Haydn, of Brahms and Bruch, of Beethoven and Schubert, of Debussy and Ravel that came flooding out of the Albis' apartment. And when he grew up, married his childhood sweetheart, Monique, and left the building, he missed the Albis' music. In the night, while Monique slept beside him, he would often remember it and think, the staircase to the fifth floor was a fabulous place to be.

It wasn't that he was musically talented himself. He had no aspirations to be good at anything like that, and what he wanted from life, apart from Monique, he wasn't really able to say.

He went to work for GDF, the national gas company. He trained as a gas fitter and began to earn the kind of salary people told him was 'decent'. He considered himself fortunate.

He liked the fact that he wore overalls to work. This meant that he could save his own clothes for Sundays, when he and Monique would go and have lunch with Madame Moutier. He was a dark, good-looking young man and he enjoyed looking smart.

Often, during those Sunday lunches, he would ask his mother if the Albis were home and felt comfortable when she said they were. Frequently, however, the Albis were in New York or Chicago or Salzburg or Adelaide. Stefan would remember all the times he'd stowed their tan-and-green luggage into the boot of the chauffeured car and the way Guido Albi would put a scrunched-up piece of blue paper into his palm – a fifty-franc note. But in all the years he'd sat on the stairs, the Albis had never seen him there. They didn't know he'd ever heard them play a single note.

Trouble came to Stefan Moutier before it came to the Albis.

He and Monique were driving down the avenue de Clichy late one Saturday night, when a garbage collection truck pulled out in front of them. Monique was thrown through the window of Stefan's new Peugeot into the maw of the truck.

Stefan got out of the car and stood in the road. He thought he was elsewhere and dreaming. He thought he was going to wake up in his bed with Monique beside him, so he just stayed still, waiting for this to happen. But it didn't happen. And from that moment, when Monique's life was thrown away, Stefan was stuck in a nightmare from which there appeared to be no exit.

The gas company were enlightened employers. They had to be because gas, after all, was a lethal product and a man who has seen his wife die in a garbage truck will need time to recover before he can be trusted with it again.

They gave Stefan Moutier a month's paid leave of absence. His colleagues held a whip-round for a large funeral tribute in the shape of an M and then they said to him: 'Stefan, nobody is capable of getting over something like this on his own. You have to have help.'

They started taking him to bars in the evenings and making sure he was well and truly drunk by the time they saw him home. He drank a variety of things: beer, pastis, vodka, cognac, whisky, rum. He admitted to Madame Moutier: 'I don't like the taste of any of them, except the beer, but I like what they do to me: they let me escape from the nightmare for a few hours.'

'All right,' said Madame Moutier, 'but take care. Your father was a drinker and couldn't stop once he'd started. Don't get so dependent on it that you won't be able to quit.'

When the month was gone, Stefan put on his overalls and returned to work.

The area manager took him aside on his first morning back. 'We hope you will be able to continue in this job, Stefan,' he said. 'But I must inform you we will be monitoring you. It's nothing personal. Just the safety measures we always apply in circumstances like this.'

Stefan wanted to say: 'There are no other "circumstances like these"! This is worse than anything ever experienced by anyone working for this company!' But he stayed silent. He didn't want to be kicked out of his job.

But then he found he couldn't *do* the job any more. His hands shook. His vision, which had always been sharp, became unreliable. One minute he would be working on a boiler component and the next he'd be staring at nothing – at a terrifying void in front of his eyes.

He tried to conceal these things. A shot of alcohol at midday seemed to steady him. But now fear had crept into his nightmare, a fear so profound there were days when Stefan had to call in sick because he just couldn't cope with the idea of work.

It was on one of these days, while he lay alone in his bed, that he switched on the radio and heard some music that he recognised. He couldn't name it. He thought it might have been by Schubert. All he knew was that it was one of the pieces he used to listen to on the stairs outside the Albis' apartment.

And it also brought him instantly to a decision: he couldn't work as a gas fitter any more. He was too afraid of what he might do, the mistakes he might make. He would give in his notice to the gas company. He would leave the apartment he had shared with Monique and which now seemed chilly and full of shadows, and return to his mother. And when the distortions of vision came, when the nightmare was at its darkest, he would pray that the Albis weren't away in New York or Adelaide, but were there on the fifth floor, playing their music behind the closed apartment doors, and then he would sit on the stairs and listen.

Madame Moutier said: 'It's all very well, Stefan, but what are you going to do with yourself all day?'

Stefan reminded his mother that there were a hundred small tasks he could usefully do in the building – from carrying down luggage, to changing light bulbs, to cleaning windows.

'All right,' she said, 'but I can't spare you much money. You'll have to rely on tips. And don't spend them on drink, or you'll have nothing.'

He *had* nothing. Nothing was exactly what he had. No wife. No job. No steady state of belonging in the world. He was alive, that was all. He could get plastered and remember what it was to laugh at a stupid joke, to feel affection towards his old friends and towards a particular café or bar. But beyond this he was as good as dead. Days and weeks and then months passed, and they seemed to go on ahead of him, or at a different pace, or somewhere else, leaving him behind.

Only once in a while did he get the feeling that he was waiting for something more to happen.

It was during this time that Guido Albi fell in love with a young Chinese cellist called Jenni Chen.

From behind the door of the Albis' apartment now came the sound of Claudette Albi's hysterical crying and the breaking of crockery and glass.

'You see, Madame Moutier,' said the neighbourhood concierges, 'disruption and trouble. Exactly as we predicted.'

And it was true: the whole building could hear the weeping of Claudette and the furious shouting of Guido. Not only the building. These noises could be heard right across the courtyard and by the optometrist on the opposite side of the street.

The fourth-floor residents came down to the concierge's rooms and declared: 'We can't sleep, Madame Moutier. Our lives are being totally disrupted. Just because they're famous doesn't give them licence to disturb the whole of the 8th arrondissement.'

'I agree,' said Madame Moutier, 'but what can I do?'

'You must talk to them,' said the residents of the fourth floor. 'You must ask them really and truly, to be quiet.'

But then, suddenly, quietness fell.

Stefan helped to stow all Guido Albi's green-and-tan luggage into the chauffeured car and he was driven away. Before he left, he gave Madame Moutier a handsome tip and apologised for the disturbance he'd caused. He said he was very sad about everything, but the apartment belonged to Claudette now and he wouldn't be coming back.

Madame Moutier looked at the stash of notes she'd been given and counted them, and gave 200 francs to Stefan. 'There you are,' she said. 'And we'll have some peace now.'

But Stefan understood that, although no sound came from the fifth-floor flat, 'peace' wasn't a word that anyone should be using. He knew what was really happening to Claudette Albi up there alone. She had been Guido Albi's wife for seventeen years. Jenni Chen was twenty-four and Claudette was forty-five. She was entering a nightmare from which there was no exit.

A year passed.

Stefan's drinking became so heavy, Madame Moutier threatened to throw him out if he didn't get a grip on himself. She knew he stole money from her purse when he went on his sprees. She also knew that whenever the residents saw him reeling home drunk, they were shocked and disgusted, and that he was putting her own future as concierge of the building in danger.

And she knew something else. Stefan sometimes reverted to doing what he had been forbidden to do as a boy: he sat on the stairs outside the Albis' apartment.

But he didn't care. He wasn't listening to Schubert or Brahms. He was just waiting for the day when Claudette would start playing the piano again. He rested his back against the iron banisters. Memories of his childhood came and went. The stairwell grew dark. Sometimes, he fell into a deep sleep.

The winter was unusually cold. Stefan told his mother that he stayed in the bars and cafés to keep warm, but she knew better. She understood now that her livelihood was definitely in jeopardy. Everything she'd worked for – on her own for all these years – was just being pissed away down the toilet.

Then, one icy morning, Claudette Albi appeared at Madame Moutier's door.

She'd wrapped herself in a black mohair shawl and her hair was wild.

She asked Madame Moutier if Stefan could come up to her flat. She said she was freezing to death up there because her boiler kept cutting out.

'Oh, I'm sorry,' said Madame Moutier, 'Stefan doesn't work for the gas company any more, Madame Albi. Not since the accident.'

'I know,' said Claudette. 'That's why I need him. I've run out of patience with the gas company. They've been round twice and this morning the boiler's cold again. I want him to sort it out.'

Stefan was still in bed, sleeping off his hangover. He shaved and dressed as quickly as he could and went up the stairs to the fifth floor. He had never been inside the Albis' apartment, never further than their little hallway to deliver flowers or crates of champagne or to collect luggage. He took with him his fitter's tool kit, unused for more than a year.

Claudette showed him into her beautiful rooms, which did feel cold, as if no one had been living in them for a long time.

'You see?' she said. 'I can't live up here like this, can I, Stefan?'

'No,' he said. 'You can't.'

She took him to the boiler and he knelt down in front of

it and opened its casing. He saw immediately that the pilot light was out and he thought that all he would need to do was relight it. But each time he tried to relight it, it extinguished itself and he had to think for a moment to remember the likely reason for this. Then he turned to Claudette, who was crouching beside him. He put his fist in front of his mouth, so that she wouldn't smell the drink on his breath.

'It's the over-ride,' he said. 'This black thing here. It's a safety device. It cuts off the gas if, for any reason, the pilot light goes out. Normally, it can be reset in order to relight the appliance.'

'Then reset it, Stefan.'

'I've tried, Madame Albi. It won't reset.'

'Well,' said Claudette, 'that's ridiculous. The gas people already fitted a new one of those black things, but this new one must be faulty too. So what am I to do?'

Stefan turned back to the boiler. He ran another test on the over-ride and found, once again, that its trigger was jumping, too soon, allowing no gas at all to be fed to the pilot. He said: 'I'm sorry, Madame Albi. The gas company will have to come back. I can't adjust the over-ride. They'll have to put in another new one for you.'

Claudette stood up. She said she would make coffee in her espresso machine for both of them. Then she said: 'Stefan, I'm tired of being cold. While I make the espresso, disconnect the stupid over-ride and get the boiler going.'

Stefan was about to say that he couldn't do this, but then he looked at Claudette, shivering and pale, and decided to stay silent.

*

He was in the apartment with Claudette Albi for about half an hour. When the radiators began to heat up, he checked them for air locks and leaks. In the music room, he saw the shutters were closed and the grand piano covered with dust sheets.

He drank the strong coffee and Claudette Albi thanked him and pressed into his hand a crumpled twenty-euro note, and then he left.

As he went down the stairs, he felt strangely happy, just as if he'd worked some miracle. And, in a small way, he had. What had been missing in those rooms was warmth and this was what his professional expertise had enabled him to supply. He thought, from now on, from this moment, perhaps Claudette Albi will start to play the piano again.

But Claudette Albi knew she would never play the piano again. She knew that a vast, unending silence had settled over her life.

She waited until nightfall. Then, she switched off the boiler and opened the glass casing that covered the gas burner. She extinguished the pilot light.

She laid her head on a cushion as near as she could get to the burner with its pinprick escape holes for the sweet and sickly gas, and moved the boiler switch to ON. Dying, she thought, is identical to living: it consists only in breathing.

Madame Moutier wanted to keep the news of Claudette Albi's death from Stefan. But it couldn't be kept from anyone. For forty-eight hours the whole building was under siege from the police and the press. Nobody thought to question the Moutiers about the defective state of Madame Albi's boiler.

Months passed. Madame Moutier knew how Stefan had admired and revered the Albis, and she was afraid this latest catastrophe would pitch him even further down into his spiral of drink and depression.

But this didn't happen. In fact, by the time the warm weather came again, Stefan Moutier seemed, at last, to be coming out of his nightmare.

It was difficult to understand exactly why. He himself wasn't absolutely certain. But he knew that losing Claudette Albi had something to do with it.

It was as if, once both the Albis were gone and he knew that no more Beethoven or Debussy would ever come out of that apartment, Stefan had over-ridden his distant past and, with it, the more recent past of his own tragedy. He had left them both behind and was now able to turn his face towards the future. In this future, he told himself, there would one day arrive a different kind of music.

# The Ebony Hand

In those days, there was a madhouse in our village.

Its name was Waterford Asylum, but we knew it as 'the Bin'.

It appeared to have no policy of selection or rejection. If you felt your own individual craziness coming on, you could present yourself at the door of the Bin and this door would open for you and the kindly staff would take you in, and you would be sheltered from the cruel world. This was the 1950s. A lot of people were suffering from post-war sadness. In Norfolk, it seemed to be a sadness too complete to be assuaged by the arrival of rock'n'roll.

Soon after my sister, Aviva, died of influenza in 1951, my brother-in-law, Victor, turned up at the Bin with his shoes in a sack and a broken Doris Day record. He was one of many voluntary loonies, driven mad by grief. His suitability as a resident of Waterford Asylum was measured by his intermittent belief that this record, which had snapped in half, like burned, brittle caramel crust, could be mended.

Victor was given a small room with orange curtains and a view of some water-meadows where an old grey-white bull foraged for grass among kingcups and reeds. Victor said the bull and he were 'as one' in their abandonment and loneliness. He said Aviva had held his mind together by cradling his head between her breasts. He announced that the minds of every living being on the earth were held together by a single mortal and precarious thing.

I had a lot of sympathy for Victor, but I also thought him selfish – selfish and irresponsible. Because he abandoned his daughter, my niece, Nicolina, without a backward glance. It was as though he simply forgot about her – forgot that she existed. Nicolina walked home from school that day and did her homework, and ate a slice of bread and jam and waited for her father to turn up. There was no note on the table, no sign of anything out of the ordinary. Nicolina fed the chickens and did the ironing, and by that time it was dark. There was no telephone in that house. Nicolina was thirteen. She'd lost her mother less than a year back. Now, she sat in that Norfolk kitchen, watching the clock tick and listening to the owls outside in the black night. She told me that she sat there wishing she were five years old once more, eating salad cream sandwiches on her mother's lap. Then she found a torch and put on her coat, and walked the two miles to my house. 'Auntie Merc,' she said, 'my dad's gone missing.'

It was a cold November. We knelt by the gas fire, wondering what to do. We made ourselves sweet drinks out of melted Mars bars and milk. We wished we had a telephone or a car. We hoped that when morning came, normal life might be resumed. But some things are never resumed, not as they have been before, and my life was one of these things.

Nicolina was too young to live on her own in an empty

house where her beautiful mother had once practised flamenco dancing and baked tuppenny silver charms into Christmas puddings, where her father had once come home from the war with gifts of nylon stockings and wind-up toys. So she stayed with me in the little brick bungalow where I'd lived alone for more years than I bothered to count. And I, who had no children of my own, or a husband, or anybody at all, tried to become a mother to Nicolina. I was forty-one years old. I had no idea how to be a mother, but I thought, well, in five or six years' time, Nicolina will find a husband and then I can hand her over to him. All I need to do is make sure this husband is a good one. I thought I'd begin looking for him right away. And until then, I'd wash her hair on Friday evenings and save up for a radiogram. I'd tell her stories about Aviva and me when we were girls. I'd show her the picture of our Spanish grandfather who owned a bakery in Salamanca. I would try to love her.

She always called me Auntie Merc. Aviva and I had both been given Spanish names and mine was Mercedes. She – who had died at thirty-six – had been christened after life itself and I – who was unable to drive – had been christened after a car. Some of the people in our village still laughed out loud when they said my name.

Despite this, I was very fond of the village and never wanted to leave it. I couldn't imagine my life as a liveable thing anywhere outside it. I had a part-time job in a haberdasher's shop called Cunningham's. I enjoyed measuring out elastic and changing the glove display on an ebony hand which stood on the counter top. When Victor said what he said about our minds being held together by peculiar things, I thought to myself that the peculiar thing, in my personal case, was this wooden hand. It was well made and heavy and smooth. I polished it with Min cream one a week. I enjoyed the way it never aged or altered. And I began to think that this hand was like the kind of man I had to find for Nicolina: somebody who would not change or die.

On Saturdays, Nicolina and I would walk down to the Bin to visit Victor. We always took exactly the same route, through the village and out the other side on the road to Mincington, then made a short cut along a green lane than ran down to the water-meadows through orchards and fields.

There was one cottage on this lane, where a young man, Paul Swinton, lived with his mother, and it was often the case that when Nicolina and I came along, on our Saturday morning visits to Victor, Paul Swinton would be out working in the cabbage fields which bordered the lane. He would stop work and raise his cap to us and we would both say 'hello, Paul' and walk on. But one Saturday, after we'd walked on, I looked back and saw him staring at Nicolina. He was leaning on a hoe and gazing at her, at her pale hair tied in a ribbon and at her shoulders, narrow and thin, beneath her old green coat. And what I saw in this gaze was a look of pure longing and infatuation. And it was then that I thought that perhaps I had found him – before I'd officially begun my search – the good husband for Nicolina, whose feelings for her would stand the test of time.

I said nothing to my niece. On we went, down the hill to the meadows where the bull trudged round and round, then up the tarmac path to the gates of Waterford Asylum, alias the Bin. We always took some gift to Victor, a jar of honey or a bag of apples. It was as if we couldn't let ourselves forget that Victor had come back from the war with his kitbag loaded up with presents cadged from the Americans. And I remember that on the day when I looked back to see Paul Swinton staring at Nicolina, we were carrying a basket of eggs.

When we gave the eggs to Victor, he took them all out of the basket, one by one, and arranged them on the windowsill in the sunshine, beside the orange curtains. 'They'll hatch out now,' he announced.

'Don't be a nerd, Victor,' I said. 'They're for eating, not rearing.'

He looked puzzled. His eyes darted back and forth from the eggs to Nicolina and me, sitting side by side on the bed, which was the only place to sit in Victor's tiny room. I looked at Nicolina, who would soon be fourteen and who was managing her life with fortitude. 'The eggs will go bad if you leave them in the sun, Dad,' she said quietly.

'No, no,' said Victor, 'your mother used to hatch eggs. In the airing cupboard. Turn them twice a day. She was full of wonders.'

Visits to Victor seldom went marvellously well. Sometimes, he seemed lost in a dream of an imaginary past. On the day of the eggs, he told us that he and Aviva had taken a cruise on the *Queen Mary* and that they had won the on-board curling championship and afterwards charvered in a lifeboat.

'What's "charvered"?' asked Nicolina.

'Dear-oh-dear,' said Victor, looking at his daughter with anguish. 'I see your mind is already turning to smut.'

'Shut up, Victor!' I said. 'If you can't control what you say, then don't talk.'

We sat in silence for a while. Nicolina took out a handkerchief from her pocket and wound it round and round her finger, like a bandage. Victor reached out suddenly and snatched the handkerchief from her hand. 'That belongs to your mother!' he bellowed.

'No . . .' said Nicolina.

'I will not put up with people appropriating her things!'

'Calm down, Victor,' I said, 'or we'll have to leave.'

'Leave,' he said, folding the handkerchief very tenderly on his knee. 'Get the fuck out of my nest.'

When we got back to my house, Nicolina sat at the kitchen table, playing with two cardboard cut-out dolls she'd had since she was nine. These dolls had a selection of cut-out clothes that could be attached to their shoulders with paper tabs: polka-dot sundresses, white peignoirs, check dungarees, purple ball gowns. Nicolina referred to these dolls as her 'Ladies'. Now, taking the dungarees off the Ladies, leaving them in their pink underwear, she said: 'I wish I was a Lady. Then I wouldn't have to visit my father any more.'

I didn't reply directly to this. But I crossed over to the table and picked up a ball gown and a paper tiara. 'These are lovely,' I said.

After her fourteenth birthday, I began to notice a change in Nicolina. She was gradually becoming beautiful.

When she came into Cunningham's, the old Cunningham sisters stared at her, like they sometimes stared at advertisements for millinery they couldn't afford. And now, every single Saturday, even when it rained, Paul

Swinton waited for us, pretending to hoe his cabbages, and we would stand and have long conversations with him about the clouds or the harvest or the ugly new houses they were building along the Mincington road. As we chatted, I would watch his brown eyes wander over Nicolina's body and watch his hands, restless and fidgety, longing to touch her.

Nicolina and I never spoke about Paul Swinton. Though I knew he would one day become her kind and immovable husband, and believed I saw, in the way she stood so still and contained in front of him, that she knew this too, it seemed too soon to mention the subject. And I didn't want her to think I was counting the years until she left my bungalow, for this was not the case. My efforts to love Nicolina were succeeding fairly well. I began making her favourite fruit crumbles with tender care. When she was late home from school, I would start to feel a weight in my heart.

One Saturday in May, Nicolina refused, for the first time ever, to come with me to visit Victor. She told me she had revision to do for her exams. When I began to protest that her father would be upset not to see her, she put her arms round me and kissed my cheek, and I smelled the apple-sweetness of her newly washed hair. 'Auntie Merc,' she said, 'be a sport.'

I left her working at the kitchen table and went on my way to Waterford and when Paul Swinton saw that I was alone, he stood and stared at the lane behind me, hoping Nicolina would materialise like Venus from the waves of cow parsley.

I had no present for Victor that day and when I told this

to Paul he took a knife out of his belt and cut a blue-green cabbage head and said: 'Take this and say it's from me and tell Victor that one day I'm going to marry Nicolina.'

A silence fell upon the field after these solemn words were spoken. I watched a white butterfly make a short, shivery flight from one cabbage to the next. I noticed that the sky was a clean and marvellous blue. Paul cradled the cabbage head in his hands. He stroked the veins of the outer leaves. 'Watching her grow and bloom,' he said, 'is the most fantastic thing that's ever happened to me.'

'I know,' I said.

'I've promised myself I won't invite her out or do anything to push myself forward until the time seems right.'

'I'm sure that's wise.'

'But I'm finding it difficult,' he added. 'How much longer do you think I have to wait?'

'I don't know,' I said. 'Perhaps until she's sweet sixteen?'

Paul nodded. I could imagine him counting the weeks and months, cold and heat, dark days and fair. 'I can wait,' he said, 'as long as, in the end, she's mine.'

With Nicolina's beauty came other things. She put her Ladies away in a box that was tied with string and never opened. She badgered me to buy the radiogram I still couldn't afford. I found one second-hand. Its casing was made of walnut and it was called 'The Chelsea'. And after that, Nicolina spent all her pocket money on Paul Anka records.

A boy called Gregory Dillon came round one teatime and Gregory and Nicolina danced in my front room to the song 'Diana'. They played the same record seventeen times. When they came out of the room, they looked soggy and wild, as though they'd been in a jungle.

'I think you'd better go home, Gregory,' I said. And he went out of the door without a murmur. It was as though dancing with Nicolina had taken away his powers of speech.

He came back a few days later, smelling of spice. His black hair was combed into a quiff, like Cliff Richard's, and his legs looked long and thin in black drainpipe trousers. He brought the record 'Singing the Blues' by Tommy Steele, but I told them to leave the door to the front room open while they danced to it. I sat in the kitchen, chopping rhubarb.

> *I've never felt more like singing the blues*
> *Cos I never thought that I'd ever lose*
> *Your love, dear . . .*

Half my mind was on Nicolina and Gregory and the other half was on the changes occurring at Cunningham's, changes which might put my job in jeopardy. The two Miss Cunninghams were retiring and there was talk of the premises being sold to a fish-and-chip bar. That day, I'd gone to see Amy Cunningham and said to her: 'If the shop closes, please may I keep the ebony hand?'

'What ebony hand, Mercedes?'

'The hand for the glove display.'

'Oh, that. Well, I suppose so. Although, if it really is ebony, then it might be valuable. It might have to be sold.'

'In that case, I'll buy it.'

'What with? You spend every penny you earn on that girl.'

I'd never heard Nicolina referred to as 'that girl' before. I hated Amy Cunningham for saying this. I wanted to give her face a stinging swipe with a tea towel. 'I'll buy it,' I repeated, and walked away.

Yet when I got home and Nicolina and I were eating our tea in the kitchen, I raised my eyes and looked at her anew, as though I had been the one to call her 'that girl', and I saw that in among her beauty there was something else visible, something that I couldn't describe or give a name to, but I knew that it was alarming.

'Nicolina . . .' I began, but then I stopped because I hadn't planned what I was going to say and Nicolina looked at me defiantly over her glass of milk and said: 'What?'

I wanted, suddenly, to bring up the subject of Paul Swinton. I wanted to remind her that his hands were strong and brown, unlike Gregory's, which were limp and pale. I wanted to reassure her that I had been thinking about her future from the moment she'd come to live with me and that my vigilance on this subject had never faltered. But none of this could be said at that moment, so I started instead to talk about the closure of Cunningham's and its replacement by a fish-and-chip bar.

'Does that mean,' asked Nicolina, 'that we'll have no money?'

I carried on eating, although I didn't feel hungry. I wanted to say: 'I suppose I knew that the young were heartless.'

It took quite a long time to complete the sale of Cunningham's, but because everybody in the village knew that it was going to close, fewer and fewer people came into the shop. It became a bit like working in a hospice for artefacts, where everything was dying. I began to feel a sentimental sorrow for the wools and bindings and cards of ric-rac. Every morning, I removed the glove from the ebony hand and dusted it. Sometimes, I held the naked hand in mine and I thought how strange it was that no man had ever wanted to touch me and that I had never had a purpose in life until I became Nicolina's replacement mother. I stood at my counter, wondering what the future held. I tried to imagine applying for a job at the fish-and-chip bar, but I knew I wouldn't do this. I didn't like fish-and-chips. In fact, I didn't like food any more at all and I saw that the bones of my wrist were becoming as narrow as cards of lace.

Not long after this, some months after Nicolina's fifteenth birthday, during a time when Elvis Presley's 'Love me Tender' wafted out all evening from The Chelsea, I arrived at Cunningham's to find the ebony hand gone.

I searched through every drawer in the shop and unpacked every bag and box in the stockroom, and then I telephoned Amy Cunningham at home and said: 'Where is the hand you promised me?'

'I did not *promise* it, Mercedes,' said Amy Cunningham. 'And, as I thought, an antique shop in Stratton is prepared to give me a very good price for it. The hand is sold.'

I stood in the empty shop, unspeaking (as people did in the novels I sometimes took out of the Mincington library). I unspoke for a long time. A customer came in and found me like that, unspeaking and unmoving, and said to me: 'Where are your knitting patterns?'

The following day, Saturday, I couldn't get out of bed. I said to Nicolina: 'I'm sorry, but you'll have to go by yourself to see Victor.'

She stood at my bedside, wearing lipstick. She offered to bring me a cup of tea.

'No, thanks,' I said. 'I'm going to go back to sleep. Give your father my love.'

'What shall I take him?' she asked.

'I have no idea,' I said. 'You're on your own today.'

She looked at me strangely. Her lipsticked mouth opened a little and hung there open and I didn't like looking at it, so I turned my face to the wall.

'Auntie Merc,' said Nicolina, 'when you're better, can you teach me the flamenco?'

'No,' I said. 'I can't. Your mother was the dancer. Not me.'


The following Saturday, when we passed the cabbage field, there was no sign of Paul Swinton. I stopped on the lane, expecting Paul to appear, but everything was still and silent in the soft rain that was falling. Nicolina didn't stop, but walked on in the direction of Waterford, holding high a pink umbrella. She looked like a girl in a painting.

When we got to the Bin, the Senior Nursing Sister pounced on us and took us into her office, which had a nice view of a little lawn, where an elaborate sundial stood. I saw Nicolina staring at this sundial while the Senior Nursing Sister talked to us, and I understood that both of us had our minds on the same thing: the sudden, swift passing of time.

The Senior Nursing Sister informed us that Victor had fallen into a depression from which it was proving difficult to rescue him. He had broken his Doris Day record into shards and thrown away his shoes. He'd cut open his pillow and pulled out all the feathers and flung them, handful by handful, round his room. I privately thought that, at that moment, he must have looked like one of those ornamental snowmen, trapped inside a glass dome.

'Why?' I asked.

The Senior Nursing Sister sniffed as she said: 'Your brother-in-law had become accustomed to watching a white bull that was kept on the water-meadows. Our staff would sometimes be aware that, instead of addressing them, as reasonably requested, he was addressing the bull.'

Nicolina laughed.

'We knew about that old white bull,' I said. 'Victor imagined—'

'The bull has gone,' said the Senior Nursing Sister. 'We enquired of the farmer as to why it had been removed from the meadow and we were told that it had been put away.'

'What's "put away"?' said Nicolina.

'Gone,' said the Sister. 'Put out of its misery.'

I looked at Nicolina. We both knew that the Senior Nursing Sister was unable to talk about death, even the death of a bull. And I thought this could be one of the reasons why so many people came voluntarily to the Bin, because, there, the words which described the things that made you afraid were differently chosen.

'We've become alarmed that Victor might inflict harm on a fellow inmate,' said the Senior Nursing Sister, 'so we have had to move him.'

'Move him where?'

'To a secure room. We hope it may be a temporary necessity.'

Neither Nicolina nor I spoke. We stared at this woman, who was unobtrusively ugly, like me. We'd brought Victor a gift of twenty du Maurier cigarettes and I knew that we wouldn't be allowed to give these to him, in case he set fire to the soft walls which now surrounded him.

'What's going to become of him?' I said.

'He's receiving treatment,' said the Sister. 'We expect him to recover.'

We had no choice but to trudge home through the rain, and when we came in sight of the cabbage field, I thought perhaps Paul Swinton would be there and that the sadness we were feeling about Victor might lift a little with his breezy smile. But when we got to the green lane, Nicolina said: 'Let's go a different way. Let's go by the road and see the new houses.' And she went hurrying on, leaving me standing still as the sun came out and cast a vibrant light on her pink umbrella.

Things began to move quickly after that day, as though striving to catch up with time.

The Chelsea exploded one afternoon, and when I rushed into the front room to see what the bang was, there were Gregory and Nicolina doing the forbidden thing on the floor behind the sofa. Flames were beginning to lick the curtains, but Nicolina and Gregory stayed where they were, finishing what they had to finish, and when I turned on the fire extinguisher, Gregory's bottom was covered with foam, like fallen feathers.

That evening, when Gregory was gone and the fire was out, I told Nicolina she ought to be ashamed of herself.

She picked her teeth and flicked what she found there on to the hearthrug. 'Are you listening to me?' I said.

'No,' said Nicolina. 'Why should I be ashamed of myself? Just because you never had a man? And anyway, I love Gregory. When I'm sixteen, we're going to get married.'

I felt very hot. I felt my blouse begin to stick to my back. 'What about Paul?' I said.

'Paul who?' asked Nicolina.

'Paul Swinton, of course. He told me he'd wait for you . . .'

'He knows that's pointless. He knows I'm marrying Gregory.'

'How does he know?'

'Because I told him.'

'Told him when?'

'That time when you were in bed. He started to say ridiculous things. I told him they were ridiculous. I told him I was soon going to be Mrs Gregory Dillon.'

I got up and went over to Nicolina. I tried to put my arms round her, but she pushed me away. 'I want better for you,' I said.

'Shut up, Auntie Merc!' she snapped. 'I'm going to get peeved with you if you crush me with stuff like that.'

In the nights, I lay in my narrow bed and wondered what to do. I thought of the life Nicolina would have with Gregory Dillon in some lonely city. I wished Aviva were alive to snap her castanets in Gregory's face and send him packing.

I contemplated trying to talk to Victor, but Victor had gone very silent since his time in the Secure Room. He sat by his window, smoking and staring at his feet in bedroom slippers. I took him a transistor radio and he held it close to his ear, like you might hold a watch, to hear its tick. He never asked about Nicolina and she never visited him any more.

And on the green lane, there was never a sign of Paul Swinton. The cabbages grew and the sun shone on them and then, one day, they were cut and gone, and the leaves and roots left behind began to smell sour. It became irksome for me to walk that way.

On my last day at Cunningham's, before the removers came to take away what was left of the sewing silks and bindings, a woman came into the shop and sat down at my counter. It was Mrs Swinton, Paul's mother. She wore a choked expression, as though she found it difficult to swallow. She blinked very fast as she talked. She asked me to persuade Nicolina to change her mind and agree to marry Paul. I invited her to sit down on one of the last remaining leather chairs. 'Nicolina doesn't know her own mind,' I said. 'She's too young.'

'No,' said Mrs Swinton. 'Paul told me she was planning to marry somebody else. Some boy.'

'She's saying that in the heat of the moment. Because they dance and carry on. But it won't last. They're children.'

Mrs Swinton stared at me sternly, no doubt wondering how I could allow my niece to 'carry on' with anybody at the age she was. In her day, said this stare, nobody carried on in this village.

She opened her bag and took out a handkerchief and dabbed her eyes, which were brown, like Paul's. 'He's so unhappy,' she said. 'I don't know what to do. He's letting the land go to ruin.'

What came into me then was a sudden white-hot rage with Nicolina for breaking the heart of the man who loved her. 'Who do you think you are?' I wanted to scream at her. 'Just tell me who.'

'I'll talk to her,' I told Mrs Swinton. 'Tell Paul to try to be patient. It may all work out in the end.'

'I hope so,' said Mrs Swinton. 'The power of love to wound is a wretched business.'

After Mrs Swinton left, I stood alone in the shop, which had always been sweetly perfumed with mothballs, until it was almost dark. Then I walked home and found Nicolina in bed, weeping.

I tried to stroke her hair, but it was in a wild tangle, as though she'd attempted to pull it out. She screamed at me to leave her alone.

I went downstairs and, out of habit, melted a Mars bar with milk to make a hot drink. I imagined I was making it for Nicolina, but then I decided she wouldn't want a Mars bar drink right now, so I stood by the stove, drinking it myself. I longed for my dead sister to come alive again and walk in my door.

I switched on the wireless and a programme about the Camargue came on: a wild place full of white horses and bulrushes and empty skies, and I thought how lovely it would be to go there, just for a day, and smell the horse smell and the salt wind. I was so caught up in the programme that I didn't hear Nicolina come downstairs. But suddenly I looked up and saw a figure at the kitchen door and jumped right out of my cardigan, imagining it was Aviva's ghost.

Nicolina was wearing old check dungarees, a bit like the

ones we used to dress her Ladies in. Her eyes were burning red.

'Gregory's gone,' she said.

'Sit down, Nicolina,' I said.

'I don't want to sit down.'

'Come on. Sit down and we'll talk about it.'

'I don't want to talk about it. He's gone. That's all. It's over. I'm only telling you because you need to know.'

She turned round then, as if to go back upstairs, but there she stopped and stared at me and said: 'There's something else. I'm pregnant. I expect you'll throw me out now. I expect you'll disown me.'

I spent the next weeks and months trying to reassure Nicolina. I told her I would repaint the little room at the back of my bungalow and make it into a nursery. I said a baby would be a novelty in my sheltered life. I said we would build a swing and hang it from the apple tree at the bottom of the garden. I said there was no chance of anybody being disowned. No chance.

Slowly, she came crawling out of her misery shell. She told me she was grateful for what I was doing. And, one Saturday morning in October, she agreed to come with me again to visit Victor.

We followed our old route over the fields. Nicolina made no protest about this. As we drew level with Paul Swinton's land, my heart began to beat unsteadily, wondering if he would be there, wondering if, when he saw Nicolina with her pregnant belly, he would try to do her harm. But there was no sign of him. The field was ploughed and empty soil. Yellow leaves from the hedgerows lay fallen there. It was as if Nicolina had known this is how it would be: just the blind earth, waiting for winter.

We went on, saying nothing, carrying our gifts for Victor, which consisted that day of some slices of cold pork and a bag of pear drops. We'd decided not to tell Victor about the baby. If you told Victor anything in advance of its being, he was unable to grasp it. It was as though the future were an enormous mathematical equation that had no meaning for him. Or perhaps time itself had no meaning for him any more. He hadn't seen Nicolina for months, but when we went into his room and she handed him the pork slices wrapped in greaseproof paper, all he said was: 'Aviva's hair was dark, but yours was always fair. I prefer the dark.'

She kissed his stubbled cheek and we sat down on the bed. Victor unwrapped the pork slices and began eating them straight away. Between mouthfuls he said: 'We've got a new resident. Younger than the rest of us. His name's Paul Swinton.'

I looked at Nicolina, but her face was turned away. She was holding on to a hank of her pale hair.

'I'm all in favour of new residents,' Victor continued, crunching on a sliver of crackling. 'They cheer me up.'

That night I couldn't sleep. Sorrow makes you weary, but never gives you rest.

I really didn't know how I was going to get through my future: the baby, the dirt and noise of it and having no money to buy toys. All I'd ever wanted was quietness. A life spent measuring elastic. I'd had forty-three years of a life I'd loved and now it was over.

The following day I took a bus to Stratton. A long time

had passed since Amy Cunningham had sold the ebony hand to the antique shop there, so I told myself that it would be gone by now. But it wasn't gone. It was standing on a marble washstand, with a price tag of seventeen shillings tied round its thumb. And when I saw it and picked it up, a surge of pure joy made my head feel light.

There was only one problem. I didn't have seventeen shillings. I said to the shop owner: 'I'll give you what I have and pay the rest in instalments.'

The shop owner had a little chiselled beard and he stroked this tenderly as he regarded me, clutching the hand to my breast. 'How much have you got?' he asked.

I counted out eight shillings. He looked at this money and said: 'I'll take eight. It was sold to me as ebony, but it's not, of course. It's mahogany. It's just gone a bit dark with time.'

He offered to wrap the hand in brown paper, but I said this wasn't necessary. I carried it away, just as it was, held tightly in my arms. And when I got home, I brought out the Min cream and a duster and polished it till it shone, as it had always shone in the Cunningham's days. Then I placed the hand by my bed, very near my pillow, and lay down and looked at it.

I asked it to give me courage to go on.

# Loves Me, Loves Me Not

Frank Baines arrived in London from the USA on a fine September morning in 1985. He put up at a hotel in Piccadilly and dozed awhile, and then he went down into the lobby and stared out at the red buses and the tides of people, hurrying along in the sunshine. And he felt wary of stepping out and joining them, because they seemed too vivid and noisy, too purposeful, knowing and bright.

Frank remembered England dark. Dark and slow and quiet. Dark railway carriages, on slow trains, where silence was preferred. Dark pubs. Dark little homes with, under the stairs, some deeper, incredible darkness in which a dog or a cat – or sometimes a child – lay sleeping. And that strange, end-of-the-world darkness that was a London wartime dusk . . .

Frank took off his glasses and rubbed his eyes. He realised now that to have gone on imagining England the way it had been in the 1940s was dumb. Years had come and gone. There had been the Beatles and Mary Quant and pale-pink lipstick. There had been Julie Christie with her shining teeth. Now, there was Mrs Thatcher in all her shades of electric blue, and her yellow hair. But Frank had only ever seen these people in magazines or on the TV, and so it was almost as though he'd never believed they were quite as they seemed, never believed they hadn't been enhanced by some clever, artificial light. Because the England that he'd once known had stayed in his mind through all these decades of change: a monochrome world, hushed and wintery and pure of heart. And it was only now, in 1985, standing in the lobby of the expensive hotel he couldn't really afford, that Frank saw how stubborn and wrong his vision of this country had been.

He stood very still, looking at the day's brightness, but not moving. People swept by him, going in and out of the revolving hotel doors. Some of them stared at him, as if they understood how painful and profound was this hesitation of his. He thought, with affection, that they might be fellow Americans, but he wasn't sure about this. Some might have been Germans.

Frank was an average-sized man with a freckled face. He'd never been handsome, but at seventy-one, his sandy hair was still wiry, his hands strong, his eyes a watery but flirtatious blue. He had a son who'd followed him into the motor trade. He had a wife, Barbara, and a white-painted house in the small town of Sweetwater, Maryland, USA. He was not unhappy. He loved his dog, whose name was Jeff.

But there was a thing that had always nagged at Frank Baines, an important event in his past which had kept on and on, through forty years, visiting his dreams. There had been an explanation for it, but Frank had never quite believed in this explanation, just as he'd never quite believed England was precisely as it appeared to be on his TV screen. He knew this was pig-headed of him, even weird, some might have said. But he just couldn't lay it to rest in his heart.

So now, at seventy-one, he'd decided – without mentioning it to a soul – that the time had come to find this rest. He got on the plane in an optimistic mood, not caring that Barbara was hurt he didn't want her along. He told her there was a War Veterans Reunion in London he wished to attend on his own, in the hopes of meeting up with a few old pals from the US 9th Armoured Division.

Frank had never been on a transatlantic airliner before. But he managed to enjoy the flight, with all the miniature things he was offered – toothpaste, whisky, nuts, socks – and the way the British flight crew pronounced the word 'sir'. When the plane landed at Heathrow, in a pale and luminous dawn, he wondered whether, at his age, he was too old to hold a stranger in his arms.

Frank walked out at last into Piccadilly, turned right and paced slowly along. The traffic, bunched up and fumy, barely moving but nevertheless travelling recklessly on the wrong side of the road, made him nervous. He suspected that he looked like a convalescent, like someone let out too soon from protective custody, and, in a way, this was how he felt. And he had no idea where he was headed. Part of him wanted not to be here.

When Frank saw the Ritz Hotel across the road, he decided he would cross over towards it, because it was a place he remembered, a place that looked as if it hadn't changed. But he saw immediately that crossing Piccadilly would be difficult. He stopped and considered what it involved, but couldn't reach a definitive answer. He imagined that the traffic lights might slow the traffic but not be certain to halt it, that there would be some code of safe behaviour understood by Londoners, but not by him.

He stood for a while at the crossing's edge, letting a girdle of other pedestrians cluster round him, and when they moved to cross, he moved with them. Despite the shield these others formed, Frank kept turning his head, left and right, left and right, right and left, right and left, to make sure he wasn't going to be run over. His heart was pounding all the while.

He considered going into the Ritz – but for what? He'd eaten what felt like five meals in a row on the plane. At his hotel, he'd gulped down some cold foreign beer. He stood in the shade of the Ritz's arches for a few minutes, gazing into the carpeted lobby, remembering some of the old music that was once played there; then he walked on. This walking on brought him to Green Park, where, though summer was past, a few deckchairs had been set out, amid the yellowing and falling leaves.

He felt grateful to see grass and trees. He sat down in one of the deckchairs with a sigh so deep it almost caused him pain. Not far from where he was, a young couple were throwing a frisbee back and forth, back and forth between each other, and Frank marvelled that each time they caught it and held it and launched it again in a perfect arc. He wanted to applaud them. Precision was a thing he'd always admired. He'd been happy in the US Army for this very reason.

Watching the frisbee, Frank felt himself gradually begin to relax and his heart slowed. With the sun warm on his face, he closed his eyes. And there she was again. As if she lived there, between his eyes and the world. His first and only love, Marie.

Marie Smythe from the village of Swallowfield, Suffolk, England. Twenty-one-year-old orphaned girl with a dimpled smile. Bare legs, even in winter. Smoked the Chesterfields he gave her with a sly smile on her face. Lay with him in the attic room of the pub where she lived and worked. Let him adore her, with her heavy breasts and her chestnut hair. Promised to be his bride when the war ended – if it ever ended, if life could ever go back to being what it once was. Swore on her dead mother's little crucifix she wore round her neck that she loved him, her Yankee boy, her big man, her wicked, wonderful Frank Baines. Said she'd follow him anywhere in the world . . .

That was the word she used. *Follow.* Even now, even after his life had had the shape it did, he could still hear it, hear it like a bell tolling.

He was twenty-nine and he'd found love. Holed up in the ice pit of Bastogne, with the US 9th Armoured Division in the winter of 1944, it had been the thought of Marie that kept him alive. No kidding. It was Marie Smythe who kept his blood circulating somehow, when his feet had turned to clods of iron, when his hands couldn't grip the rifle butt. But for her, but for his memory of what had happened between them in that attic room and the promises they'd made, he would have lain down in the snow and died. Instead, he tried to write letters to her on scraps of frozen paper: *Marie, we're going to have a fine life. Wait till you see the tulip trees in Sweetwater!* These letters didn't describe the hunger of Bastogne, the dead of Bastogne, the impenetrable ground. They described the future. *Build us a house with a porch and paint it white. Raise us a big family. Call our firstborn Jeff, after your poor father . . .*

Frank's familiar reverie was interrupted by the arrival of

a person in uniform, who told him he couldn't sit in the deckchair unless he bought a ticket for it. Disorientated, Frank said he wasn't going to stay in the deckchair, but the attendant insisted that he would nevertheless have to pay for the time he'd already spent in it.

Frank looked up at a young face, pallid and wan. 'Son,' Frank heard himself say, 'do you know anything about the war?'

'What war?' said the attendant.

*What war.* Frank now felt a tirade rise in his throat, words about American lives laid down, but just before the tirade came out he thought, well, OK, there was Vietnam.

He reached in his wallet for a five-pound note, handed the note to the attendant, thought to himself, that's when things must have changed here, not right after the war, but then. After Vietnam, the whole world was different.

'I can't change this,' said the attendant, after scrabbling in a leather bag. 'Give me something smaller.'

'I don't have anything smaller,' said Frank. 'I just came from the airport.'

'Jesus Christ!' said the attendant. 'You're my third bloody Yank today. Have the fucking chair free.'

Frank took back his money. He felt confused and dizzy. All he longed to do now was sleep.

In the spring of 1946, Frank returned to Sweetwater and, with the help of his widowed mother, Hazel, bought a plot of land. His knowledge and experience of US Army tanks helped him find a job repairing cars. He moved in with Hazel, not far from where his land lay waiting for the house of his dreams to be built on it.

Then, he sent for Marie.

The moment when Marie Smythe would walk down the gangway of the ship and into his arms seemed such a momentous one that he felt he had to rehearse it in his mind long before it arrived. So this is what he began to do. He saw it as a kind of film, which he described to his workmate, Sol.

'I guess it's near dawn, Sol,' he said. 'I'm in New York City and I'm at the waterfront early. And there's some fog or mist in the air and it's cold and I can see my breath.'

'Fog and mist?' said Sol. 'Why fog and mist?'

'Dunno. But there they are. Then I pan out over the water. It's like the world ends there, in the mist, you know? Like they used to believe the world had an edge.'

'Nuts,' said Sol. 'You're nuts, Frank.'

'OK, but that's how it feels. And then I hear it, that old ghostly siren. You know? That boom-boom of a big ocean liner, and so I know she's there and coming closer. And then the scene fills up. There's a crowd all round me, stamping in the cold, shouting, kids throwing stuff, waving flags. There's a band playing.'

'Would there be a band?' interrupted Sol.

'Who knows? There's one in my mind. And I'm jigging up and down. I can't keep still. Maybe it's the cold or the excitement, or both. I've got the ring in my pocket. And I hold on to it like it's the crown jewels.'

'You didn't buy the ring yet, did you?' said Sol.

'No, but I'm asking around. I think I can get a deal I can afford on a solitaire.'

'Diamond?'

'Sure, diamond. What else?'

'She might be OK with an opal.'

'No, she wouldn't. This is love, Sol. This is my future wife, Marie. Opals are definitely not coming into it.'

Sol, who'd been married for fourteen years, was a sceptic. He was also undereducated and forgot that the word had a 'c' in it, so he said to Frank: 'I'm a septic, Frank. I don't believe things are ever the way you picture them.'

But they were the way Frank had pictured them – more or less.

By the time Marie embarked on the ship, he'd bought the diamond solitaire and he looked at it every night of the ten nights of her journey. He had his sandy hair cut and his suit cleaned and his best shoes shined. He helped Hazel prepare the chaste and tiny room where Marie would sleep, until they were man and wife. He placed a picture of himself in his army uniform by her narrow bed. Nostalgia for the 9th Armoured Division overcame him for a moment or two, then went gradually away.

He drove to New York City in an ancient Chevy he'd repaired and made good as new. On a grey morning of freezing mist, he made his way through the unfamiliar streets to the waterfront. There, he waited. A US Navy band was playing. He heard the siren and saw the great booming ship slide towards him out of the milky light. He began to jig up and down, shouting: 'Marie! Marie!'

The passengers disembarked, smiling, waving. One by one, they were swept into the arms of the crowd and led away into the tall, beautiful city. The band played on and on, then suddenly stopped and the day fell silent. All the passengers were gone and Marie was not among them.

It was dark, now, in Frank's hotel room. Without meaning to, he'd slept the day away and now it was evening.

He called Barbara and told her he'd arrived safely, but that London had gotten brash, crowded and confusing.

'Well,' said Barbara Baines, 'times change, Frank. Nothing stands still.'

He asked after Jeff. Barbara told him that Jeff had lain on the porch all day, waiting for his master to come home. Frank hung up soon and ordered a steak from Room Service.

He turned on the TV and saw Mrs Thatcher, wearing her Pacific blue, addressing some awesome gathering, against a billowing blue backdrop. All the men on the podium behind her were smiling anguished smiles, as though at some adored and disdainful lover. Older women can be sexy, thought Frank. When I see Marie tomorrow, I may still feel that I want to touch her body.

He listened to Mrs Thatcher's speech for a while but didn't take in much of what she said, just enjoyed the sound of her voice. And he remembered how, in Marie's attic room above the pub, he would ask her to talk to him, say anything, tell a story, no matter what, just keep on talking in that soft, English voice of hers until he fell asleep. At Bastogne he heard her still, in the howling cold, in the star-filled nights. She called him 'darling'. She whispered to him that he would survive, that the war would be won. 'Keep holding on, Frank Baines,' she told him. 'Bastogne will be relieved.'

She was right about Bastogne. There was an end to all their suffering. But why had she kept him alive? What for? He thought she'd wanted him as her husband and then, in the end, she just slipped away into darkness, as though she'd never ever been in his life.

Back in Sweetwater, he'd told Sol: 'That day in New York, it stayed dark, you know. The sky just never seemed to lighten, not even for an hour.'

'That figures,' observed Sol. 'There are times like that.'

But these times were incomprehensible. What happened next was worse, or at least as bad as waiting on the waterfront for Marie: her trunk was delivered at Hazel's apartment.

The address on the label – Hazel's address – was written in Marie's round handwriting, and Frank had the sudden notion that this girl had played an outrageous game with him and that she was – like Cleopatra, delivered to Caesar in a rolled-up carpet – inside the trunk.

He put his arms round the trunk and called her name. Hazel lit a cigarette and told her son not to be macabre.

He got out his army knife and picked at the locks until they gave. Inside the trunk were all the clothes he knew Marie Smythe to possess. Wrapped in tissue paper were nylon stockings he recognised as his own gift and a silky nightdress the colour of peach ice cream. He held this garment against his face and wept.

His mother, who was seldom moved by anybody's tears, said: 'There's something odd here, Frank. Why would she send her clothes and not follow them? I think she must have been detained on the ship.'

'Detained why?' he sobbed.

'I don't know, dear. Maybe she committed a felony.'

'Marie? A felony? Like what?'

'Don't ask me. It's all a mystery. Maybe she cheated at cards on board? Or . . .'

Frank wiped his eyes on the peach nightdress. 'Or what?'

'Perhaps you didn't wait long enough and now she thinks you've abandoned her.'

'No,' he said. 'I told you. I waited for five hours.'

And he had. This was why the day never seemed to lighten. He let time pass and pass. He pestered the people from the shipping line. He told them her name, demanded to see the purser. And this man arrived at last and told Frank no, nobody of that name was on the voyage. Nobody called Marie Smythe.

But now the trunk had turned up. Marie had packed everything she owned. Surely these clothes had been laid in there by the future Mrs Frank Baines?

Hazel looked sorrowful and said: 'You know, Frank. Maybe she was sick and couldn't be moved off the boat. Or maybe she died at sea.'

He called Sol then and said: 'I saw this in the war, Sol. The British don't like to talk about death.'

'Nah,' said Sol. 'They would of told you. Or you'd of gotten a cable.'

'Not necessarily. I'm not Next of Kin, yet.'

So then, the thought of her dying and her body being cast into the ocean and her chestnut hair tangled among the fishes of the deep made him cold and shivery. He couldn't sleep. He knelt by the trunk and unpacked Marie's possessions, one by one. At the very bottom of the trunk was a framed photograph of her parents, which Frank held close to his body for a long time.

Later, a letter came.

It asked Frank to forgive her. It enquired politely whether he would be able to ship her possessions home to England, because these things were all she had. It gave no explanation, only said that she'd changed her mind *at the last minute*. And she was sorry, she knew promises had been made, important promises, but sometimes promises were impossible to keep and that was the way of the world. She sent him her love and hoped his future would go well.

So then, not on bits of frozen paper, but on a large yellow pad, Frank poured out his fury. He told Marie she'd ruined his life. He said he wished now he'd died at Bastogne. He tore the peach nightdress to shreds, tied the nylon stockings in knots with which he wanted to strangle her.

Sol kept saying, with his wisdom of fourteen years of marriage: 'You'll get over it, Frank. Everybody gets over everything in the end. There's no such actual thing as a broken heart.'

But – perhaps it was the war, perhaps it was Bastogne and staying alive for her sake, or perhaps it was just the way Frank turned out to be – the truth was that he'd *never* quite gotten over it. And in recent times, a man in his seventh decade now, this had begun to drive him crazy. He felt he'd wasted his life. Why couldn't he forget something that happened forty years ago?

He'd got to thinking lately that he'd never gotten over it because of the damn trunk. If the trunk had never arrived, perhaps he would have made better headway with his career, been able to give more of his heart to Barbara, more to his son. But that trunk had always and always bothered him. The tender care with which Marie had laid that nightdress in . . .

He lay sleepless beside his wife in the dark and thought: just suppose Marie *was* on the ship after all? Just suppose, when the liner docked, she was standing at the rail, looking forward to seeing me, Frank Baines, her future husband, longing to disembark and rush into my arms. And then, when that mist lifted, when she saw me there, saw me jigging up and down in that stupid way that I was, she thought, no, I can't do it, I can't marry that moron, that sandy-coloured American who doesn't pronounce my name right. I can't let my destiny be joined with his.

And so what did she do then? She hid on the ship. She stowed away. Did she? Or perhaps not? Perhaps she ran crying to the purser. Bribed him to say she wasn't on the passenger list, if anyone should enquire. Bribed him with what? Bribed him with her body, the body that had been given to Frank in a lightless room in Swallowfield, with an owl calling outside in the dark? And then sailed right on back to England a few days later, with all the crew knowing who she was, the girl with chestnut hair, who'd sold herself to the purser for a lie . . .

Once there in his mind, this new explanation wouldn't leave Frank Baines a moment's peace. He'd lived with the idea of himself as some kind of hero, a man who had risked his life for Europe and who was, in consequence, owed lifelong respect in that part of the world. But now he saw himself as Marie had seen him that day: an insignificant American, childish in his gestures, a person who was going to spend his life repairing stinking automobiles.

He felt himself sinking into perpetual misery. Even his walks with Jeff took on a sad aspect. His love for this dog now struck him as a tragic thing.

So he sat down and wrote to Marie. He had no idea if her old address in Swallowfield would find her. He asked her to come to London and meet him for dinner at a hotel of her choice. And after three or four weeks, a reply turned up. He recognised her writing on the envelope straight away. A few things about a person never change, he observed, and handwriting is one of those few.

A night and a day passed.

Frank was now sitting in the hotel lounge, where a harpist played. A waiter brought him the tea and sand-wiches that he'd ordered, but he didn't really want any of this. He felt nervous, slightly sick. Just over three hours remained before his meeting with Marie and, to his mild surprise, this meeting was suddenly taking on the aspect of an ordeal. Frank sat and counted the cost of the plane ticket, the cabs, the hotel, the drinks and meals. He thought of Jeff lying on the porch and waiting for his master and whining as the night came down.

Why had he arranged the trip at all? Only to hear confirmed the sorry truth that his English fiancée had sailed to America, taken one look at him and sailed back. But why in the world had he assumed Marie would ever admit to this? She was a woman of sixty-three. She would have learned some skill with people's feelings by now. He could already hear her saying: 'No, no, Frank. You've got that completely wrong. I just . . . in the end . . . couldn't leave England, that was all. I never got on the ship.'

And then they would eat their expensive dinner and talk of other things. Other things of no importance. And after that, after a liqueur, a green liqueur, say, she would leave. He would watch her go, a middle-aged Englishwoman getting thick around the waist, her chestnut hair gone grey, a person who had been afraid to leave the shelter of her village, for whom the idea of America had been too challenging and pitiless and bright.

'God dammit to hell!' Frank said aloud and some of the

other people taking tea turned round to stare at him, and even the harpist looked up at him over the strings of her harp as he threw his linen napkin down and strode out of the room.

Just after eight o'clock, the phone in Frank's room began its summons. He knew he had only to pick it up to hear a voice announce to him that a Miss Marie Smythe was waiting for him in the lobby downstairs. But he let it ring.

It rang three more times, at five-minute intervals. And then everything went quiet again.

He felt peaceful, lying on the hotel bed, more peaceful than he'd felt in a long time. He poured himself a whisky from the minibar.

London, England, flickered and rumbled and churned outside his window, but he had no interest in it. None. Let it go its unfathomable way. Why should any American care about one single thing in it? Why should any American in his right mind ever have cared?

As he drank the good whisky, Frank Baines began wondering how long he had left to live. Five years? Ten? He hoped it might be ten. He hoped, when the dog died, there'd be time for one more pet and that, in the scented Sweetwater evening, Barbara would say: 'I suppose we're going to call him Jeff once again, are we, Frank?'

And Frank would say no.

# Moth

I was her new neighbour on the Sunny Lawns Trailer Park, that's all. The park was a mile or two out of Knoxville in some nice country, with a lake and a cluster of live oaks.

Everybody called her Pete. I dunno what name she got at her baptism. That's her secret. She was Pete to us all. Nobody said OK, but what's your real name?

She was on her own with two kids, a girl and then a boy who was just a baby. The thing she loved to do was called appliqué. She'd learned it from some sewing magazine. You cut up shapes of fabric, preferably shiny, and you machine them on to things, to make patterns. That's appliqué. If you get tired of making patterns, you can make pictures – like a girl in a bonnet, or a bluebird.

Day and night, night and day Pete sat in her trailer doing her appliqué. Her sewing machine got so hot it wouldn't let itself be touched. She made laundry bags and cushion covers and aprons, and sold them up in the Smoky Mountains somewhere, in a craft village. There was a flaked-out hippie in that village who had a thing for her. He made rustic fencing and his hair was grey as a waterfall. Pete and he lay on the floor of his cabin, lit by oil lamps, but she wouldn't let him do it to her. When I imagine this scene, I put a poster of Yoko Ono on the wall above, wearing her dark glasses.

The father of the kids used to work for the Fire Service. Still does, I guess. You could dial 911 in Knoxville and still get him to fight your fire. His name was Chester and he had an appetite so big, he used to snatch food off Pete's plate and stick it in his own mouth. He weighed down the trailer. And his shit wouldn't flush away, it was that huge. Apparently. Pete would have to take a hoe and break it up like you break up the dirt of the yard after the winter frost.

Yet I guess she loved him. That's one of the odd things about it all. She loved Chester and never minded breaking up his shit with a hoe or letting him grab the bacon off her plate. But then he left her for a girl of twenty-two and this she did mind. That's when she took up the appliqué. If I'd been her, I would have imagined I was sewing Chester's foreskin on to his face, stitching up all his lying orifices, but I don't know what her reason was precisely. All she said about it was: 'Annie, never again will I put my trust in one single thing.'

Her little girl, Lisa, was five and as good as apple pie. She came to visit me and we'd make popcorn and Lisa'd hold tight to the long-handled pan and say, 'Wow!' She had a whispery laugh, like the wind in the grasses at the edge of the lake, and her favourite singer was Mary Chapin Carpenter.

She never mentioned her daddy. I guess Pete told her not to think about him any more, because he didn't seem to figure in her mind at all. Whenever she slept over at my trailer – when Pete went to sell her appliqué and get herself fondled by the mountain hippie – Lisa would say her prayers and leave the cheatin' ole firefighter out of them completely: *God bless Mom and Baby Ricky and All the Poor People everywhere, Amen.*

And then she'd sing herself to sleep with the words of Country songs. Her little thin arms would wave around in the cot, in time to the beat, and then suddenly she'd go quiet and never wake till morning. She was the only human being I've ever met who could go to sleep with her arms sticking straight up in the air. Sometimes, I'd lay them down by her sides, or sometimes I'd just leave them the way they were.

Baby Ricky was different from Lisa from the start. Pete told me when he was born he weighed so heavy the scales emitted a bleep, like a warning. He was Chester's boy. Pete tried to suckle him as she'd suckled Lisa, but she told me: 'I couldn't go on with it, Annie, Ricky'd pull at the nipple so hard. So I weaned him and put him on a full bottle. He'd fill his diapers and as soon as I'd changed him he'd yell out for more, dammit, and some days I had to feed him twenty times in twenty-four hours and all I had of sleep was a few minutes here and there.'

She got him on solid food and he quietened down. That's when Chester left – in one of those quiet times when Baby Ricky was full of food and lying in his pram, staring at the ceiling of his trailer home, and Pete was dead asleep. Who knows if he looked at Baby Ricky one last time and said 'see ya, kid', or if he was just in such a sweat to get out of there that he never gave his son a glance? It makes no difference. It's just a habit I have, trying to imagine the details of things, like I put in that Yoko Ono poster in the hippie's cabin. Anyways, Chester was gone, leaving Pete with those two kids, Lisa and Baby Ricky, and her sewing machine. And it was soon after that I moved into the trailer next door to them and Pete and I became friends.

I was on my own. I worked in a dry-cleaners called Secco's where all the bagged-up clean stuff on its hangers got rotated round the back room on a moving rail and all the employees got rotated round the different machines, to keep them alert.

Some days, I stood in the back window, operating the presser and watching the Tennessee spring bust out of the redbud trees and out of the earth. A lot of the clothes I pressed had moth holes or scorch marks in them and weren't worth cleaning. I daydreamed I'd write a book before I was forty. I guess the heat from the presser and the scent from the frothy redbuds mingled together to give me this grand illusion, because now my fortieth has come and gone and there's no sign of my book, only this true story of Pete and Lisa and Baby Ricky. So I'm going to put this all down. Everything happened real fast, but in a way it was long and complicated, like a book can be.

I guess Ricky was about nine or ten months old when Pete said to me: 'Annie, there's something wrong when I lay Ricky down because he kicks and screams like he's in pain, but I don't know why.'

I said to take him to the doctor's, Pete, but she said no, she wouldn't yet, she hated going there and waiting in line and breathing the germ-filled air, and anyway doctors these days didn't know shit. I had to agree with her there.

So I helped her to examine Ricky. We put him on a

blanket and undressed him and held him up and looked at him, limb by limb. He reminded me of a sumo wrestler. He wouldn't keep still. He wanted to be on his knees, crawling around among the scraps of satin under the appliqué table. His body felt hot and there was a glisten of sweat in the fold of his neck, but his eyes were bright as tin and his skin was rosy and there was no bruise or scratch on him. But then we tried to lay him on his back and when his shoulders touched the floor he screamed so loud Lisa came running in from the dusty yard and stood in the doorway watching.

Pete picked him up and, real gently, trying to make my hands as soft as gloves, I touched his back and then I said to Pete: 'I can feel something here, Pete, where his shoulder blades are, I can feel two lumps there.'

'Jesus Christ!' said Pete. 'Lumps? Where?'

I showed her and she pressed them with her fingers and Ricky screamed.

'Couldn't be cancer,' said Pete. 'One on either side like that. Couldn't be, could it?'

'No,' I said.

'Guess I'd better take him by the doctor, had I?'

'Or you could wait. See if they just go.'

'Yeah. They could go. Could be the way he keeps trying to pull himself up with his arms, like it's made his muscles swell, could it?'

'Dunno,' I said. 'I never studied anatomy.'

Then one night I was lying asleep after my long day at Secco's when Pete came thumping on my trailer door.

'Annie,' she said, 'come quick. Ricky's on the ceiling.'

I said what did she mean 'on the ceiling' and she said come see.

I got into my dressing gown and followed Pete into the room where the two kids slept. Lisa was awake and sitting on her bed, staring up. And just as Pete had said, there was Ricky, wearing a diaper but nothing else, looking down on us from on high. It was like he was full of helium and had floated up there like a balloon. He wasn't holding on to anything and he wasn't one bit afraid. He was gurgling with happiness and little gobs of his spittle plopped down on to our heads, like rain. It was the weirdest thing I'd seen in thirty-nine years of living.

Lisa said: 'I want to go up on the ceiling too!'

So I said: 'Sweetheart, hold on a minute, because we don't know how Ricky got there and the ceiling ain't that good a place to be.'

Pete said: 'Annie, since Chester left, I jes' dunno what in the world is goin' on.'

And I said: 'Well, Pete, maybe Ricky's practising being a firefighter, spittin' on us, like that,' but no one laughed.

Then I got a chair and climbed up on to the old teak wardrobe where the kids kept their things. I didn't feel that safe up there. I felt too heavy for the furniture. I wasn't far from where Ricky was, so I steadied myself and reached for him, but no sooner had my hand touched him than he spun away from me, going in a zigzag towards the light fixture.

'Jesus Christ!' said Pete.

'Ricky's flying!' said Lisa.

And we could hear a miniature sound as he moved, a kind of whirring, like from a portable plastic fan you can buy to keep your face cool on a June day.

We had to move the wardrobe three times before I could get Ricky, because he didn't want to be got. He wanted to go on zooming around up there out of everyone's reach. But I caught him in the end and handed him down to Pete, and he began screaming louder than we'd ever heard him scream before. He tried to struggle out of Pete's arms, but Pete held on to him and wouldn't let him go and that's when she started swearing Jesus Christ Jesus Christ and went real pale, and Lisa stuck her thumb into her mouth, and I climbed down and knelt by the side of them.

Growing out of Ricky's shoulder blades in the place where I'd found the lumps was a pair of wings. They were the colour of Ricky's pink flesh and there was blood on them and they were bedraggled and small, but they were wings all right, and after a long struggle with Pete, Ricky got them palpitating fast like the wings of a hummingbird and he flew out of the bedroom door into the bright, watery light of the kitchen.

I said to Pete: 'We oughta let someone look at these wings, like a surgeon for example.'

But Pete said: 'No way! We're keeping them hid and pray they drop off.'

Then a few days later I said: 'Listen, Pete, you know this is a phenomenon unique in the world – the flying baby! All you gotta do is advertise and charge for entry and let Ricky fly around the trailer park, and in one month you'll be a billionaire.'

This got her thinking. Instead of keeping Ricky's wings folded away all the time inside his clothes, she let him use them to fly round the trailer. He liked to hover near the ceiling and he got dirty from all the dust and grease up there, but you could tell he was happy. Except he was lousy at landings. He had to fall down and roll over like a parachutist and this crushed his wings every time and there seemed to be no way to soothe the pain that he felt. We tried putting wych-hazel on his feathers, but it didn't do anything and soon after Pete said to me: 'Annie, for nine-tenths of his life that child's in mortal agony.'

Pete was still considering becoming a billionaire with my flying baby idea, but she said she was going off it because really she couldn't believe – after what happened with Chester – that any human plan could turn out right. She said: 'Annie, why can't everything just be safe and ordinary like it was before?'

I said: 'Pete, this is one crazy time we're alive in. When was anything safe and when was it ordinary?'

Pete said: 'I guess you're right. It never really was.'

We were in Kroger's supermarket in Knoxville when we had this conversation, with Ricky in our shopping cart and Lisa trailing along with a little carton of mango juice.

Pete and I were examining the thirteen different kinds of salad leaves you could buy at Kroger's, looking at all their names like arugula and radicchio and lollo rosso that never used to be part of life on earth. We were so caught up with the arugula that we forgot about Ricky for one entire minute and when we looked round at him, he'd tugged off his T-shirt and was pulling himself up, and before we could grab ahold of him he'd started his hummingbird thing and lifted off above the vegetable display. He hovered there for a moment, then went flying away down the supermarket aisles.

We just stood there. We couldn't think what else to do. And we saw all the shoppers struck dumb one by one and stand real still, gawping and pointing. In his usual way,

Ricky had gone up to the ceiling which, in Kroger's, was chequered with big panels of light. And I shall never as long as I live forget the sight of him crossing these light panels and casting sudden little shadows across the store. I know a lot of people in Kroger's that day just didn't believe what they were seeing. They thought Ricky was an electric baby, operated by remote control.

We waited and watched and there was no sign of Ricky coming down. He was in his element up there. So I went to the manager and said: 'Sir, what I suggest is you switch off the overhead lights and then maybe he'll decide to land.' So in a moment or two the store went dark, except for the fluorescent tubes above the food counters, and we all called to Ricky and held out our arms, and in a while he came circling down and landed in a box of apples.

Now, the local press and then the national press and then the international press crammed into the trailer park. You couldn't go out or come in because of all the ladders and tripods and people and Styrofoam cups of coffee and slabs of cold pizza and discarded paper tissues. Pete and I and Lisa sat in the dark of Pete's trailer, pretending we weren't there, and reading the offers of money from the media that were stuck under the door.

'You were right, Annie,' said Pete. 'I guess I could get rich now.' And so we began thinking about all the things she could buy, if she took one of these offers, like a nice home not too far from Kroger's and a leatherette couch and a doll's house for Lisa and a dog with brown eyes.

Pete was about to come to a deal with ABC news, to let them film Ricky flying round the trailer ceiling, when Chester arrived. He barged his way through the journalists and cooed at Pete through the window, saying: 'Honey, I love you and I was wrong to leave, so let me in, doll, because I want to come back to you.'

I said: 'Pete, don't listen. All he wants is Ricky.' But the sight of Chester's huge face at the window seemed to be more than she could resist, so she opened the door and in he came, all two hundred fifty pounds of him, and he took her to him and stuck his tongue in her mouth and held her ass in his fat hand.

Then he saw me. 'Who's this?' he said.

And Pete said: 'No one, just Annie.'

'Tell her to get out,' he said, 'and take Lisa. We need some privacy here.'


I know what happened next, but I dunno if I've got everything in the right order. I guess Chester screwed Pete so hard that afternoon that her brain stopped functioning. I guess she let him make any deal that came into his mind, provided he swore he'd never leave her again.

Press guys came and went from Pete's trailer. I held on to Lisa and we made a salad that was five colours of red and green. Towards evening, Chester came out, holding Ricky in his arms, the proud father, and all the photographers went flash flash and Chester held Ricky up to the TV cameras to show the world his feathers.

Then they followed him and Ricky down to the cluster of live oaks at the north corner of the park. It was getting close to sunset, so they got some big lamps and shone them up into the trees. Pete was there, but hanging back out of sight. Lisa and I tried to get to her, but we were cut off by the crush of people and cameras so I said to Lisa: 'Don't worry, sweetheart, I guess everybody just wants to see Ricky flying around under the oaks and then they'll be satisfied and go home and things will be back to normal.'

She said: 'What if he won't come down, Annie?'

And I said: 'Don't worry, kid, Ricky came down in Kroger's, remember, he came towards the light.' And I guess we were both thinking about the way Ricky had landed in among the fruit when we saw him go.

The crowd gave a gasp like they do at a NASA launch and there he was, flying higher and higher, and I could see insects in the light beams fluttering upwards, like they wanted to join him on his journey to the dusty trees.

Well. That was in summer and it's winter now and the bare branches of the redbuds are grey with frost.

Lisa refuses to go to school, so she comes with me to Secco's, where it's warm, and the manager, Mr Borzoni, lets her help sort out the clothes by colour and fetch water for the steam presser. It's lucky he's Italian and has compassion. I bring him chocolate, out of gratitude.

He knows the story. Everyone around here does. What no one knows, including me, is what was in Ricky's little heart that evening when, instead of flying near the tree ceiling, he made for the open sky and disappeared from view. I think it must have been that he saw the shimmer of the lake. The light was almost gone, but even at dusk there's some brilliance left on the water and Ricky flew towards that, and no one ever saw him again. They sent frogmen down into the depths to search for his body with its baby wings, but that lake is deep and they never could find it.

So I guess what Pete said to herself was that if no one

could bring him back to her, she'd just go and try to be wherever he was. I dunno. I've stopped trying to guess what was in her exhausted mind. Chester was gone too, back to the young girl's bed with his bank account stuffed with media dollars. So perhaps she killed herself because of this and not because of Ricky. I'll never know. All she said to me by way of warning was: 'Annie, if anything happens to me, take care of Lisa and don't let Chester take her away.'

They dredged Pete up. She had her sewing machine roped to her waist. Some bitch on the trailer park said it was a waste of a good machine. But what got me was the thought of all that appliqué she'd done, all those hours and hours of working at one consoling thing and how this just hadn't been enough.

We had a little ceremony for her and some of the TV people came, but fewer than those who came to see Ricky the Flying Baby. There was no sign of any mountain man with a grey waterfall of hair.

Lisa cries for Pete. I stroke her forehead and hold her close and call her my angel. My angel falls asleep with her arms sticking straight up in the air and gently I lay them down.

*The Cherry Orchard*, with Rugs

I was wearing a blossom-white suit that day. No tie. My number on the Eurostar train was seat 19, coach 04.

It rained all through Kent, but when the train pulled clear of the tunnel, there was a cold February sun shining on the grey earth of northern France. I caught sight of a church steeple, which looked turquoise on the far horizon and, in my usual (some would say banal) way, I had a fashion thought: that particular turquoise was the perfect new colour for my kitchen walls. This cheered me more than I can tell you. I laid back my head and wished I were in First Class, with greater calm and comfort to enfold me as visions of my transformed culinary environment began to pleasure my mind.

I've always adored transformations. I was born (thirty-four years ago) Darren John Sands and at work, in the carpet department of Peter Jones, people call me Darren or Daz. But I have other personae I can adopt without difficulty. One of these is a Cuban or Mexican sort of person, named Diego. I'm a good mimic and I speak a little Spanish. I have no difficulty pronouncing the word '*cerveza*' correctly. My hair is naturally thick, dark and shiny, and sometimes, if I'm in a Diego mood, I risk gluing on to my baby-soft upper lip a pencil-thin moustache, which certain types of submissive men find devastating in its lethal little way. The only thing I dread, when I'm Diego, is meeting an actual Cuban and being accused of wounding and disrespectful racial impersonation. I have absolutely no desire to wound. I become Diego to amuse myself and to enable me to meet different types of people.

When I go to Paris – which I do as often as I can afford to – I usually travel as Daniela. Daniela is the antithesis of Diego. Some people find this female persona too extreme for their tastes. I once had a lover called Bernard who hated Daniela so much, he tore a silver earring out of my ear and threw it down a drain in Wimpole Street. My ear was bleeding and I was in terrible pain. I said: 'My God, Bernard, now I'm going to die in agony, like Elizabeth Barrett Browning!' But Bernard, who never laughed at any joke of mine, just walked off and bagged the only cab with its light on in the whole colossal darkness of the Marylebone night. I was left alone, shivering and in shock, and with half my ear hanging down in shreds.

But I didn't abandon Daniela. I abandoned Bernard. And today, there I was, Paris-bound, as *she*. My make-up is always restrained: brown eyeliner, with just a smidgen of mink shadow; a lovely matt foundation on my flawless, studiously exfoliated skin and a pale lipstick, never gloss. My hair I gel into a kind of gamine Audrey Hepburn style and then just finish off the effect with some good jewellery: sometimes one, sometimes two earrings, depending on my mood. I like silver a lot. I buy the real thing from PJ's, using my Staff Discount.

I should explain that I never take Daniela to extremes. I don't wear a padded bra or try to disguise my Adam's apple with polo-necks. I'm not impersonating a woman in any comprehensive way. Not at all. The delight of being Daniela lies, precisely, in the ambiguity I strive to create. And then I watch the world look at her and wonder. I move through my universe with the perfume of people's astonishment following me like a scented cloud wherever I go. And this scent is addictive. Because, as Daniela, I know that I'm totally beautiful. And how often, in a human life, does one experience the absolute beauty of one's own being? I ask you. Not often at all.

In Paris, then, city of bridges, city of love, I like to walk around as Daniela. Do you blame me? But the train was still quite far from its marvellous destination when I had my encounter with Ross.

It was a chance thing. I'd wandered down to the buffet for a caffe latte. Ross was there, smoking. When he saw me, he inhaled an enormous *gorgé* of smoke and started to cough. The cough was horrendous. Everybody began staring. I asked the steward for an Evian water and took this over to Ross with my latte and poured it out for him, and he sipped it gratefully.

He was a gingery kind of man, with freckles on his hands. I put his age at about forty-three. His eyes were blue and trusting, and his lashes long and pale. He wore a wedding ring on his left hand and I could imagine the kind of wife he had, whose laundry smelled of Comfort, who ate boiled sweets on car journeys, whose hair might even be permed.

When he'd recovered from his coughing fit, I said, in my soft Daniela voice: 'I'm sorry if I upset you.' I touched his sleeve.

'No,' he said. 'No. But thanks for the water. Let me pay you back.'

He counted out some English money and I took it. I didn't want him to be in my debt in any way. I considered moving away and having my latte at another table, but I was enjoying the effect Daniela was having on Ross and thought I'd just see how far I might be able to take her. At my back, I could feel the stares of the other people in the buffet; their outrage, and their yearning.

Ross was a schoolteacher. His subjects were drama and English. He was travelling to Paris, alone, to see a production of *The Cherry Orchard* at some small theatre where the actors worked for nothing.

'Why do they work for nothing?' I asked.

Ross explained that they did this for the amazing experience of being directed by somebody called Patrice Boniano, a shit-hot French director who liked to 'break everything down into its simplest components, to – in Chekhov's own words – "rid the theatrical experience of everything that's petty and unreal".'

I ingested the dregs of my latte. I wanted to say to Ross that, when people utter sentences like the one he'd just pronounced, I feel they're living in some parallel universe where the air is too murky to be breathable. But I didn't say this. I said: 'Oh. I've never seen *The Cherry Orchard*. Is it marvellously good?'

'Yes,' said Ross. 'I think it is. Chekhov described it, when he finished the play, as a "light comedy", and it seems a very simple story, but there's such feeling and passion underneath. It's not really light comedy at all.'

'I love ambiguity,' I said. 'It sounds so fascinating.'

I caught, then, the tremble of a smile on Ross's mouth and he looked away from me, out at the tranquil fields of Normandy, all ploughed and harrowed and ready for the spring.

'What are the "simplest components", then?' I ventured.

'Well,' said Ross. 'It's a bit of a steal from something done by Peter Brook some years ago at the Bouffes du Nord. They're using rugs.'

'How do you mean?' I asked.

'Well, no scenery. Bare stage. Rugs on the walls and as furniture and probably as the views from the window, the views of the orchard itself.'

'How is that going to work?'

'I'm not sure. But there's an intricacy to the design of beautiful carpets which mirrors the intricacy in the text. Also, they're probably woven by slave labour in Afghanistan or Turkey, and this also feels right for what Chekhov is saying in this play about the idle aristocracy and their long years of owning serfs.'

'Oh,' I said, 'it sounds so interesting. In my very small way, I know a lot about rugs.'

'You do?' said Ross.

'Yes. I work in the carpet department at Peter Jones.'

Now, Ross laughed. He didn't mean to laugh *at me*. I don't think he did. This burst of laughter just came out in a kind of involuntary way. And the words 'Peter Jones' did sound somehow embarrassing when juxtaposed with the words 'Peter Brook'. But, immediately, I pretended to be very hurt. Daniela is excellent at this. She can almost cry at will. I looked down into my empty latte cup. I wiped a fleck of foam from my lip with a French-polished nail. Though I didn't look at Ross, I could tell that he was mortified and his laughter was replaced by a heavy silence.

'Well,' I said, after I'd let the silence go on for a while. 'I'd better be getting back to my seat.'

I looked up at Ross. His face was pink and his eyes deliciously bright.

'Listen,' he said. 'I don't suppose you'd like to . . . I don't suppose it would interest you to come with me to see *The Cherry Orchard*?'

We drank Pernod in the crowded theatre bar. Ross was wearing a soft blue mohair jacket and a black shirt, buttoned all the way up. He looked nice. For the first time, Daniela thought that she would like to lie in his arms.

The auditorium itself was very small and the rows of seats set too close together, so that we sat with our knees sticking up. Four knees, side by side. I tried to concentrate on *The Cherry Orchard*, but I had some problems. It was in French and my French is round about the B-minus grade. I think a lot of what Ross had called 'the underlying complexity' of the play was lost on me. I couldn't help finding most of the characters annoying, and quite soon I was sympathising with the businessman, Lopakhin, who wants everybody to grow up and go away.

And then there was the question of the rugs. At work, I'd been in charge of Oriental Layout and I can honestly say that the way Patrice Boniano arranged and then rearranged the rugs on the set of *The Cherry Orchard* was never, to me, as aesthetically pleasing as the way I'd arranged them in Peter Jones's carpet department. And this distracted me. I thought, I'm no one and he's a supposed genius, but I have an infinitely more subtle understanding of colour groupings.

I was quite relieved when the play was over and we walked into a small but buzzy little restaurant and Ross ordered Chablis and oysters.

Ross began to talk about Chekhov's death in 1904.

I said: 'Isn't that weird. Today, on the train, I was sitting in coach 04, seat 19,' but Ross ignored this. He told me that when Chekhov came on stage after the first performance of *The Cherry Orchard*, he was so moved by the audience's reaction that he was seized with a fit of coughing and this fit turned out to be the beginning of the end of his life.

'How was that?' I asked.

'He was ill from that moment on,' said Ross. 'A few months later, when he was dying, the doctor said to him: "I'm going to put ice on your heart," but the playwright said: "You don't need to put ice on an empty heart."'

I ate an oyster. When I dabbed my mouth, I saw a darling little smudge of pink left on the napkin. I said to Ross: 'What about you? Is your heart empty?'

'I don't know,' he said.

I reached over and took his hand and I felt it burning.

Back in my room, I asked Ross to undress me. He laid the blossom-white suit on a chair.

When I was almost naked, Ross said: 'I can't do this.' And he began to cry.

I stroked his hair. I said: 'Ross, if I understood it properly, one of the things that play's about is longing. Am I right? And the way people don't face up to what they know is true.'

Ross nodded. He kept on crying. I put on a silk robe and sat quietly by the window, listening to the intimate sounds of the Paris night.

After a while, Ross stood up and put on his overcoat. I remembered it was St Valentine's Eve. I said to Ross: 'Why don't you kiss me before you go?'

I never saw him again.

When I went back to work and looked at the rugs, they kept reminding me of *The Cherry Orchard*, as if the play had been something marvellous and signficant and over-whelming in my life. I prattled on about it until my work colleagues got completely fed up. One day, the manager of the carpet department took me aside and said: 'Daz, for pete's sake shut up about Chekhov. Just concentrate on the business in hand.'

# The Dead Are Only Sleeping

When the telephone call came, Nell was cleaning out the parrot's cage. The parrot itself had alighted on a window-sill and was pecking the glass.

'It's Laurel,' said Laurel's voice from long ago. 'It's your stepmother.'

Nell said nothing, only waited and kept her eyes fixed on the parrot.

'Nell?' said Laurel. 'Are you there?'

'Yes,' said Nell.

And then came the statement. Laurel made it quickly, in a tight whisper, as though saying it could damage her vocal cords: 'I rang to tell you your father died.'

The room where Nell stood, with the white telephone and the grey parrot, was high and light, with a shiny wood floor: a place where a person could feel calm and unconstrained.

'When?' asked Nell.

'This morning,' replied Laurel. 'I wasn't there. No one was there.'

Now, Nell sat down on a cotton upholstered chair and lightly touched the fabric of its arms. Her thought was, from now on, the world may seem a kinder sort of place.

*

Yes, but what if it wasn't true? Laurel had said no one had
been there to see it. What if another call came, cancelling
out the first? What if a trainee nurse had gone in and
mistaken sleep for death? And suppose now, as they
manoeuvred her father on a trolley into the lift and down
into the basement morgue, he was just lying there
dreaming? Because even death would surely have been
afraid of him and kept its distance until he was old and
weak, wouldn't it? So he must be fooling death and fooling
the hospital staff. When the temperature dropped as they
laid him on the slab, he was going to wake up.

All Nell could do was wait. She finished clearing out the
parrot's cage and replenished the feeder with seed. She
took the bird off the windowsill and stroked its head. It
muttered to her. This-and-that. This-and-that. But it was
the only sound. The phone didn't ring. Laurel had asked
politely: 'Would you like to come home for the funeral?'

Home? What a word to use, when Nell hadn't been
near that house for years, when her thirtieth birthday was
only a few months away and the flat she shared with the
parrot held everything she owned. She'd told Laurel she
would think about it. But then, the idea that her father
wasn't really dead made her determined to be there, to see
for herself. For only if she *saw* would she know that this
was death and not a game of the same name.

It was a Saturday morning. Earlier Nell had washed
and polished the wood floors, and now the flat smelled
scented and clean. In a moment she would call Laurel
back (brassy Laurel with her solarium tan and her beaky
nose designed to sniff out the currency value of every last
item in the world) and say: 'I'll come this afternoon. I want

to see him.' But first, Nell walked into her kitchen and poured herself a glass of cold white wine. She took a deep drench of it and found the taste so sweetly satisfying that she smiled. Smiled and drank again. Outside the kitchen window, in the top of a chestnut sapling, some London bird was warbling in the gentle April sun.

Her father's house on the outskirts of its northern city had always seemed large to Nell. Too large. As though for every room there had to be an invisible occupant, a person whose space this rightfully was. As a child, she'd searched for these people – behind curtains or in old wardrobes – or thought she heard them (yearned to hear them) talking together on the landing. She had a name for them: the Clusters. She dreamed of them crowding in to her attic, dressed in white. They would tell her: 'Here we are, dear. Don't be scared. And look who's with us: your mother! She's woken up at last.'

Now, as Nell drove north, she decided she would refuse Laurel's offer to stay overnight. What her attic room contained these days was Laurel's exercise equipment: rowing machines, cycles and weights. It had become a kind of gym where middle-aged Laurel's sinew and muscle were toned, to keep her young and fighting fit. So where, in the huge house, would she sleep anyway, if her attic was a fitness centre? Not in what her father called the Old Room, the bedroom he'd once shared with Nell's mother. And all the Cluster rooms had functions now: computer room, games room, solarium. There would be no space for her in any of them. No bed.

And for years, anyway, the very idea of the house had been loathsome to her: its stale-fruit smell, its way of seeming dark. No, she'd find a cheap hotel nearby and perch there. A narrow bed, a TV within reach. Or perhaps she wouldn't even stay the night, but turn straight round and drive back to London? All she needed to verify was the incontrovertible fact of her father's death. She certainly didn't want to lay flowers on the mound. She wasn't going all this way to forgive him.

The house was full of people she'd never met: Laurel's friends. They stood about in the kitchen, searched cupboards for teacups and sugar and packets of biscuits. When Laurel introduced her, they turned from whatever they were doing to look at her. 'Did he have a daughter?' said their stares. 'How peculiar that we never knew.'

Nell took the cup of tea she was offered and, as though drawn by some remembered physical routine, began to make her way up the stairs towards her attic.

'Nell,' said Laurel's voice behind her, 'wait a moment. Don't you want to talk?'

Nell didn't pause, but went on up. 'No,' she said. 'And I'm not staying. I only wanted to look at my room. Then I'm going to see him.'

'Listen,' said Laurel, 'if you're blaming me because he never got in touch . . .?'

'I'm not blaming you,' said Nell. 'I didn't *want* him to get in touch. I wanted to forget.'

'You know he mellowed . . .' began Laurel.

'I don't know anything,' said Nell.

Laurel was standing on the half-landing (the very place where the gentle Clusters used to whisper), her tanned face looking lean, her white angora sweater crackling with the electricity of sudden shock. Nell turned her back and climbed the remaining stairs to the attic. In London, the day had been sunny, but here the sky was heavy and sudden squalls of rain blew in from the west.

There was still a bed in the attic room. Or, not a bed exactly, but a kind of couch covered with a towel where, Nell presumed, Laurel rested between sets of exercises.

Nell went to it and sat down and stared at all the body equipment. Then, suddenly tired after her drive, she put her cup of tea down on the floor, drew up her feet on to the couch and closed her eyes. The couch was where her own bed had been, under the window. Twenty-four years ago, she'd been lying right here on a spring night when her father's sister, Aunt Iris, had come tiptoeing in and knelt down on the floor, with her arms resting on a chair. She had looked very pale. Nell had wondered if this aunt imagined the chair were a toilet bowl and that she was about to be sick into it. 'Nell,' said Aunt Iris, 'something has happened to your mother. And I'm the one who has to tell you.'

Nell asked Iris if she was feeling sick, but she said no, not sick, pet, only sad. And then she explained that Nell's mother had been hit by a car and, after this terrible hitting, she had fallen asleep. Fast asleep for ever. And she was never going to wake up.

Five-year-old Nell didn't believe her aunt. In the early morning, she crept down to the Old Room, expecting to find her mother lying there beside her father, but there was no one in the room and after searching for her father, she discovered him snoring on the kitchen floor. She woke him and asked: 'Is it true my mum's gone to sleep?'

The father put his two fists in front of his eyes. 'Yes,' he said. 'It's true.'

'Where?' asked Nell.

But there had never been any answer to this – not one she could remember. So, just as she searched for the Clusters, Nell began to look for her mother in the kinds of places where people might decide to go to sleep. One of these places was a shop called the Reliant Bed Centre. She would tug her hand away from the aunt and go running in. 'She's not there, love,' somebody would say. But one day, Nell saw her. She was lying on one side of a big Reliant Bed and next to her, on the other side of it, a man was lying, and Nell's mother and this man were bouncing on this bed – not asleep at all – and laughing. But then, it wasn't her; it was a stranger. 'Come away, Nell,' said Aunt Iris, 'she's not anywhere on this earth.'

Nell almost dozed, sensing the light at the window altering. She knew it was time to visit her father.

They asked if she was family. As she answered them, she choked on something – a microscopic living organism or a particle of dust from a hospital blanket – and they mistook this choke for anguish. They spoke to her kindly then and said that, when she'd been in to see him, there'd be a cup of tea waiting. This was all she'd had that day: white wine and tea.

'What was the cause of death?' Nell asked.

They didn't have the answer in their minds or to hand. They had to go away and consult a chart. Then, looking at the chart and not at her, they explained the term myocardial infarction: a blocking of the major arterial vessels, these vessels becoming stuffed with a fatty substance, restricting blood movement and eventually causing the heart to stop.

'Is it certain?' she asked.

'Is what certain?'

'Death.'

'Well, not invariably. Because there are warning signs and modes of surgical intervention that can prolong life, such as arterial bypass or . . .'

'No,' said Nell. 'What I mean is, is my father really dead?'

They looked up sharply from their charts. As if she'd just announced the closure of the hospital. 'Yes,' they chorused. 'Yes.'

Naturally, it was very cold where he lay. A white room. Two slabs, the other one vacant. Screens around him, moved aside to let her in. Cruel light falling on to his face, boring into it, giving a deep contour to wrinkles and blemishes. Nell didn't touch him, couldn't bear to reach out to him; only stared and stared, allowing herself to acknowledge the fact at last: this is no longer him, this is a corpse.

So sad, Nell had always thought them, the dead. Gone to nowhere, like her mother. Searched for and longed for and never found. But all Nell could feel for this dead body was shame, untempered by pity. The man had died of a petrified heart – his perfect end. Because it was his inadequate human heart that had sent his first wife out into a spring night, hit on the mouth, confused, weeping, wandering off the pavement and into the road when the car had come by. This same inadequate heart had taunted and bullied his only child across eighteen years of life, seeming to wish her dead each day, until the last of the last days, when she packed and left for London. And never came back. It had hardened her own heart, let her be stranded at thirty, high up in an airy empty flat with seldom the least shadow of any other arriving or departing: only the grey parrot, turning on its perch and trying to speak.

Nell lay in the narrow hotel bed. She longed for silence, but traffic on some sodium-lit throughway burdened this silence, as if it were endlessly attempting to reach her and endlessly prevented.

Would the small hours let it come? Nell doubted it. City traffic sighed and shuddered night and day, never dying down.

After two hours, Nell counted out three herbal sleeping tablets and swallowed them. She knew the sour taste they left in her mouth was from the Valerian they contained. *Valeriana officinalis*. The plant alchemised earth into bitterness and the bitterness ushered in oblivion.

And now, this oblivion was waiting near, almost ready to take her, and, as it did, Nell found herself once again in the shop where she used to search for her mother. She walked slowly up the carpeted pathway between the brand-new beds. And there she was at last, the parent who had loved her, curled up neat and comfortable on a Reliant Deluxe Pocketed Sprung Mattress. On the mother's sleeping face was a smile and when Nell reached out to touch her, the hand she held was soft and warm.

The following day Nell drove back to London. She played loud music in the car. She felt light, reckless, full of hope, as though she might still have been a girl, with all her life to come.

# Peerless

His parents had christened him Broderick, but for as long as he could remember, he'd always been known as 'Badger'. He spent his life feeling that Badger was a fatuous name, but he couldn't stand Broderick either. To him, the word 'Broderick' described a *thing* – possibly a gardening implement or a DIY tool – rather than a human being. Becoming an animal, he decided, was better than remaining a thing.

Now, because he was getting old, it worried Badger that the hours (which, by now, would have added up to years) he'd spent worrying about these two useless names of his could have been far better spent worrying about something else. The world was in a state. Everybody could see that. The north and south poles, always reliably blue in every atlas, now had flecks of yellow in them. He knew that these flecks were not printers' errors. He often found himself wishing that he had lived in the time of Scott of the Antarctic, when ice was ice. The idea of everything getting hotter and dirtier made Badger Newbold feel faint.

Newbold. That was his other name. 'Equally inappropriate,' he'd joked to his future wife, Verity, as he and she had sat in the crimson darkness of the 400 Club, smoking du Maurier cigarettes. 'Not bold. Missed the war. Spend my days going through ledgers and adding up columns. Can't stand mess. Prefer everything to be tickety-boo.'

'Badger,' Verity had replied, with her dimpled smile, with her curvy lips, red as blood, 'you seem bold to me. Nobody has dared to ask me to marry them before!'

She'd been so adorable then, her brown eyes so sparkly and teasing, her arms so enfolding and soft. Badger knew that he'd been lucky to get her. If that was the word? If you could 'get' another person and make them yours and cement up the leaks where love could escape. If you could do that, then Badger Newbold had been a fortunate man. All his friends had told him so. He was seventy now. Verity was sixty-nine. On the question of love, they were silent. Politeness had replaced love.

They lived in a lime-washed farmhouse in Suffolk on the pension Badger had saved, working as an accountant, for thirty-seven years. Their two children, Susan and Martin, had gone to live their lives in far-off places on the other side of the burning globe: Australia and California. Their mongrel dog, Savage, had recently died and been buried, along with all the other mongrel dogs they'd owned, under a forgiving chestnut tree in the garden. And, these days, Badger found himself very often alone.

He felt that he was waiting for something. Not just for death. In fact, he did nothing much except wait. Verity often asked him in the mornings: 'What are you going to do today, Badger?' and it was difficult to answer this. Badger would have liked to be able reply that he was going to restore the polar ice cap to its former state of atlas blue, but, in truth, he knew perfectly well that his day was going to be empty of all endeavour. So he made things up. He told Verity he was designing a summer house, writing to the children, pruning the viburnum, overhauling the lawnmower or repairing the bird table.

She barely noticed what he did or didn't do. She was seldom at home. She was tearing about the place, busy beyond all reason, trying to put things to rights. She was a volunteer carer at the local Shelter for Battered Wives. She was a Samaritan. Her car was covered with 'Boycott Burma' stickers. Her 'Stop the War in Iraq' banner – which she had held aloft in London for nine hours – was taped to the wall above her desk. She sent half her state pension to Romanian Orphanages, Cancer Research, Greenpeace, Friends of the Earth, Amnesty International, Victims of Torture and the Sudan Famine Fund. She was never still, always trembling with outrage, yet ready with kindness. Her thick grey hair looked perpetually wild, as though desperate hands had tugged it, in this direction and that. Her shoes were scuffed and worn.

Badger was proud of her. He saw how apathetic English people had become, slumped on their ugly, squashy furniture. Verity was resisting apathy. 'Make every day count' was her new motto. She was getting old, but her heart was like a piston, powering her on. When a new road threatened the quiet of the village, it was Verity who had led the residents into battle against the council – and won. She was becoming a local heroine, stunningly shabby. She gave away her green Barbour jacket and replaced it with an old black duffel coat, bought from the Oxfam shop. In this, with her unkempt hair, she looked like a vagrant, and it was difficult for Badger to become reconciled to this. He felt that her altered appearance made him seem stingy.

The other thing which upset Badger about the new Verity was that she'd gone off cooking. She said she couldn't stand to make a fuss about food when a quarter of the world was living on tree bark. So meals, in the Newbold household, now resembled post-war confections: ham and salad, shop-bought cake, rice pudding, jacket potatoes with margarine. Badger felt that it was unfair to ask him to live on these unappetising things. He was getting constipated. He had dreams about Béarnaise sauce. Sometimes, guiltily, he took himself to the Plough at lunchtime and ordered steak pie and Guinness and rhubarb crumble. Then he would go home and fall asleep. And in the terror of a twilight awakening, Badger would berate himself for being exactly the kind of person Verity despised: apathetic, self-indulgent and weak. At such times, he began to believe it was high time he went to see his Maker. When he thought about heaven, it resembled the old 400 Club, with shaded pink lights and waiters with white bow ties and music, sad and sweet.

One spring morning, alarmingly warm, after Verity had driven off somewhere in her battered burgundy Nissan, Badger opened a brown envelope addressed to him – not to Verity – from a place called the Oaktree Wildlife Sanctuary. It was a home for animals that had been rescued from cruelty or annihilation. Photographs of peacefully grazing donkeys, cows, sheep, geese, chickens and deer fell out from a plastic brochure. Badger picked these up and looked at them. With his dogs, the last Savage included, Badger had felt that he had always been able to tell when the animals were happy. Their brains might be tiny, but they could register delight. Savage had had a kind of grin, seldom seen, but suddenly there in the wake of a long walk, or lying on the hearthrug in the evenings, when the ability to work the CD player suddenly returned to Verity and she would put on a little Mozart. And, looking at these pictures, Badger felt that these animals (and even the birds) were in a state of contentment. Their field looked spacious and green. In the background were sturdy shelters, made of wood.

Inside the brochure was a letter in round writing, which began:

> *Dear Mr Newbold,*
> *I am a penguin and my name is Peerless.*

At this point, Badger reached for his reading glasses, so that he could see the words properly. Had he read the word 'Peerless' correctly? Yes, he had. He went on reading:

> *. . . I was going to be killed, along with my mates, Peter, Pavlov, Palmer and Pooter, when our zoo was closed down by the Council. Luckily for me, the Oaktree Wildlife Sanctuary stepped in and saved us. They've dug a pond and installed a plastic slide for us. We have great fun there, walking up the slide and slipping down again. We have a good diet of fish. We are very lucky penguins.*
>
> *However, we do eat quite a lot and sometimes we have to be examined by the vet. All of this costs the Sanctuary a lot of money. So we're looking for Benefactors. For just £25 a year you could become my Benefactor. Take a look at my picture. I'm quite smart, aren't I? I take trouble with my personal grooming. I wasn't named 'Peerless'*

*for nothing. Please say that you will become my Benefactor. Then, you will be able to come and visit me any time you like. Bring your family.*

*With best wishes from Peerless the Penguin.*

Badger unclipped the photograph attached to the letter and looked at Peerless. His bill was yellow, his coat not particularly sleek. He was standing in mud at the edge of the pond. He looked as though he had been stationary in that one place for a long time.

Peerless.

Now, Badger laid all the Sanctuary correspondence aside and leaned back in his armchair. He closed his eyes. His hands covered his face.

Peerless had been the name of his friend at boarding school. His only real friend.

Anthony Peerless. A boy of startling beauty, with a dark brow and a dimpled smile and colour always high, under the soft skin of his face.

He'd been clever and dreamy, useless at cricket, unbearably homesick for his mother. He'd spent his first year fending off the sixth-formers, who passed his photograph around until it was chewed and faded. Then, Badger had arrived and become his friend. And the two had clung together, Newbold and Peerless, Badger and Anthony, in that pitiless kraal of a school. Peerless the dreamer, Badger the mathematical whiz. An unlikely pair.

No friendship had ever been like this one.

'Are you aware, Newbold, that your friend, Peerless, has been late for games three times in three weeks?'

'No, I wasn't aware, sir.'

'Well, now you are. And what do you propose to do about it?'

'I don't know.'

'I don't know, sir!'

'I don't know, sir.'

'Well, I think I know. You can warn Peerless that if he is ever – *ever* – late for cricket again, then I, personally, will give *you* a beating. Do you understand, Newbold? I am making you responsible. If you fail in your task, it will be you who will be punished.'

Peerless is in the grounds of the school, reading Keats. Badger sits down by him, among daisies, and says: 'I say, old thing, the Ogre's just given me a bit of an ultimatum. He's going to beat me if you're late for cricket practice again.'

Peerless looks up and smiles his girlish, beatific smile. He starts picking daisies. He's told Badger he loves the smell of them, like talcum powder, like the way his mother smells.

'The Ogre's mad, Badger. You realise that, don't you?' says Peerless

'I know,' says Badger. 'I know.'

'Well, then, we're not going to collude with him. Why should we?'

And that's all that can be said about it. Peerless returns to Keats and Badger lies down beside him and asks him to read something aloud.

'. . . *overhead – look overhead*
*Among the blossoms white and red*—'

\*

207

When Verity came back that evening from wherever she'd been, Badger showed her the photograph of Peerless the Penguin and said: 'I'm going to become his Benefactor.'

Verity laughed at the picture. 'Typical you, Badger!' she snorted.

'Why typical me?'

'Save the animals. Let the people go hang.'

Badger ate his ham and salad in silence for a while; then he said: 'I don't think you've got any idea what you've just said.'

There wasn't a moment's pause, not a second's thought, before Verity snapped: 'Yes, I do. You're completely apathetic when it comes to helping people. But where animals are concerned, you'll go to the ends of the bloody earth.'

'Perhaps that's because I am one,' said Badger. 'An animal.'

'Oh, shut up, Badger,' said Verity. 'You really do talk such sentimental bollocks.'

Badger got up and walked out of the room. He went out on to the terrace and looked at the spring moon. He felt there was a terrible hunger in him, not just for proper food, but for something else, something which the moon's light might reveal to him, if he stayed there long enough, if he got cold enough, waiting. But nothing was revealed to him. The only thing that happened was that, after ten or fifteen minutes, Verity came out and said: 'Sorry, Badger. I can be a pig.'

Badger wrote to Peerless and sent his cheque for £25. An effusive thank-you note arrived, inviting him to visit the Sanctuary.

It wasn't very far away. But Badger's driving was slow, these days, and he frequently forgot which gear he was in. Sometimes, the engine of the car started screaming, as if in pain. It always seemed to take this screaming engine a long time to get him anywhere at all. Badger reflected that if, one day, he was obliged to drive to London, he would probably never manage to arrive.

He drove at last down an avenue of newly planted beeches. Grassy fields lay behind them. At the end of the drive was a sign saying 'Welcome to Oaktree Wildlife Sanctuary' and a low red-brick building with a sundial over the door. It was an April day.

At a reception desk, staffed by a woebegone young man with thick glasses, Badger announced himself as the Benefactor of Peerless the Penguin and asked to see the penguin pool.

'Oh, certainly,' said the young man, whose name was Kevin. 'Do you wish to avail yourself of the free wellingtons service?'

Badger saw ten or eleven pairs of green wellingtons lined up by the door.

He felt that free wellingtons and new beech trees were a sign of something good. 'Imagination,' Anthony Peerless used to say, 'is everything. Without it, the world's doomed.'

Badger put on some wellingtons, too large for his feet, and followed the young man across a meadow where donkeys and sheep were grazing. These animals had thick coats and they moved in a slow, unfrightened way.

'Very popular with children, the donkeys,' said Kevin. 'But they want rides, of course and we don't allow this. These animals have been burdened enough.'

'Quite right,' said Badger.

And then, there it was, shaded by a solitary oak, a grey pond, bordered by gunnera and stinging nettles. At one end of it was the slide, made of blue plastic, and one of the penguins was making its laborious way up some wide plastic steps to the top of it.

'So human, aren't they?' said Kevin, smiling.

Badger watched the penguin fall forwards and slither down into the muddy water of the pond. Then he asked: 'Which one's Peerless?'

Kevin stared short-sightedly at the creatures. His gaze went from one to the other, and Badger could tell that this man didn't know. Someone had given the penguins names, but they resembled each other so closely, they might as well not have bothered. It was impossible to distinguish Pooter from Pavlov, Palmer from Peter.

Badger stood there, furious. He'd only sent the damn cheque because the penguin was called Peerless. He'd expected some recognisable identity. He felt like stomping away in disgust. Then he saw that one of the penguins was lying apart from all the others, immersed in the water, where it lapped against the nettles. He stared at this one. It lay in the pond like a human being might lie in a bed, with the water covering its chest.

'There he is,' said Kevin suddenly. 'That's Peerless.'

Badger walked nearer. Peerless stood up and looked at him. A weak sun came out and shone on the dark head of Peerless and on the nettles, springy and green.

'All right,' said Badger. 'Like to stay here a while by myself, if that's OK with you.'

'Sure,' said Kevin. 'Just don't give them any food, will you? It could be harmful.'

Kevin walked away over the meadow where the donkeys wandered and Badger stayed very still, watching Peerless. The other penguins queued, like children, for a turn on the plastic slide, but Peerless showed no interest in it at all. He just stayed where he was, on the edge of the pond, going in and out, in and out of the dank water. It was as though he constantly expected something consoling from the water and then found that it wasn't there, but yet expected it again, and then again discovered its absence. And Badger decided, after a while, that he understood exactly what was wrong: the water was too warm. This penguin longed for an icy sea.

Badger sat down on the grass. He didn't care that it was damp. He closed his eyes.

It's the beginning of the school term and Badger is unpacking his trunk. He's fourteen years old. He lays his red-and-brown rug on his iron bed in the cold dormitory. Other boys are making darts out of paper and chucking them from bed to bed. Peerless's name is not on the dormitory list.

The Ogre appears at the door and the dart-throwing stops. Boys stand to attention, like army cadets. The Ogre comes over to Badger and puts a hand on his shoulder, and the hand isn't heavy as it usually is, but tender, like the hand of a kind uncle.

'Newbold,' he says. 'Come up to my study.'

He follows the Ogre up the polished main stairs, stairs upon which the boys are not normally allowed to tread. He can smell the sickly wood polish, smell the stale pipe smoke in the Ogre's tweed clothes.

He's invited to sit down in the Ogre's study, on an old

red armchair. And the Ogre's eyes watch him nervously. Then the Ogre says: 'It concerns Peerless. As his friend, you have the right to know. His mother died. I'm afraid that Peerless will not be returning to the school.'

Badger looks away from the Ogre, out at the autumn day; at the clouds carefree and white, at the chestnut leaves flying around in the wind.

'I see,' he manages to say. And he wants to get up, then, get out of this horrible chair and go away from here, go to where the leaves are falling. But something in the Ogre's face warns him not to move. The Ogre is struggling to tell him something else and is pleading for time in which to tell it. I may be 'the Ogre', says the terrified look on his face, but I'm also a man.

'The thing is . . .' he begins. 'The thing is, Newbold, Peerless was very fond of his mother. You see?'

'See what, sir?'

'Well. He found it impossible. Her absence. As you know, he was a dreaming kind of boy. He was unable to put up any resistance to grief.'

That evening, Verity made a lamb stew. It was fragrant with rosemary and served with mashed potato and fresh kale. Badger opened a bottle of red wine.

Verity was quiet, yet attentive to him, waiting for him to speak to her. But for a long time Badger didn't feel like speaking. He just felt like eating the good stew and sipping the lovely wine and listening to the birds fall silent in the garden and the ancient electric clock ticking on the kitchen wall.

Eventually, Verity said: 'When I said what I said about you letting people go hang, Badger, I was being horribly thoughtless. For a moment I'd completely forgotten about Anthony Peerless.'

Badger took another full sip of the wine, then he said: 'It's all right, darling. No offence. How were the Battered Wives?'

'OK. Now, I want you to tell me about the penguins. Are they being properly looked after?'

He knew she was humouring him, that she didn't care one way or the other whether a bunch of penguins lived or died. But the wine was making him feel cheerful, almost optimistic, so he chose to say to her: 'The place is nice. But the penguin pool's not cold enough. In the summer, they could die.'

'That's a shame.'

'I won't let it happen. I've got a plan.'

'Tell me?' said Verity.

She poured him some more wine. The stew was back in the oven, keeping warm. Mozart was softly playing next door. This was how home was meant to be.

'Ice,' said Badger. 'I'm going to keep them supplied with ice.'

He saw Verity fight against laughter. Her mouth opened and closed – that scarlet mouth he used to adore. Then she smiled kindly. 'Where will you get that amount of ice from?'

'The sea,' he said. 'I'll buy it from the trawlermen.'

'Oh,' she said. 'Good idea, Badger.'

'It'll be time-consuming, fetching it, lugging it over to the Sanctuary, but I don't mind. It'll give me something to do.'

'Yes, it will.'

'And Peerless . . .'

'What?'

'He seems to suffer the most with things as they are. But the ice should fix it.'

'Good,' said Verity. 'Very good.'

He lined the boot of his car with waterproof sheets. He bought a grappling hook for handling the ice blocks. He christened it 'the Broderick'. Despite the sheeting, Badger's car began to smell of the sea. He knew the fisherman thought he was a crazy old party.

But at the pond, now, when the penguins saw him coming, lugging the ice on an ancient luge he'd found in the garage, they came waddling to him and clustered round him as he slowly lifted the end of the luge and let the ice slide into the water. Then they dived in and climbed up on to the ice, or swam beside it, rubbing their heads against it. And he thought, as he watched them, that this was the thing he'd been waiting for, to alter the lot of someone or something. All he'd done was to change the water temperature of a pond in the middle of a Suffolk field by a few degrees. As world events went, it was a pitiful contribution, but he didn't care. Badger Newbold wasn't the kind of man who had ever been able to change the world, but at least he had changed this. Peerless the penguin was consoled by the cool water. And now, when Verity asked him what he was going to do on any particular morning, Badger would be able to reply that he was going to do the ice.

From this time on, in Badger's nightmares, the death of Anthony Peerless was a different one . . .

Peerless has come to stay with him in Suffolk. There

are midnight feasts and whispered conversations in the dark.

Then, one morning, Peerless goes out alone on his bicycle. He rides to the dunes and throws his bicycle down on to the soft sand. He walks through the marram grass down to the sea, wearing corduroy trousers and an old brown sweater and a familiar jacket, patched and worn. It's still almost summer, but the sea is an icy, meticulous blue. Peerless starts to swim. His face, with its high colour, begins to pale and pale until he's lost in the cold vastness. He floats serenely, silently down. He floats towards a vision of green grass, towards the soft smell of daisies.

> . . . *overhead – look overhead*
> *Among the blossoms white and red.*